Used to life on the street, Finn never expected to be hired by a magician after saving him from a rival street gang—let alone a magician with a penchant for book hoarding and performing occasionally-exploding experiments. But Master Kestrall is a kind-hearted man, even if he sends Finn on far too many errands to the bookstore. After all, Finn is infatuated with Jonti, the master bookkeeper's handsome apprentice. The only problem is, Finn has absolutely no experience in matters of the body and no idea how to go about acting upon his feelings. That all changes when, on one of his regular trips to the Crow's Nest, Finn brings home a certain book that holds some very rare knowledge indeed—and when Finn accidentally-on-purpose summons an incubus into his midst, nothing will ever be the same again.

The Apprentice's Incubus
Copyright © 2021 Diana Waters
ISBN: 978-1-4874-3013-9
Cover art by Martine Jardin

Published by eXtasy Books Inc or
Devine Destinies, an imprint of eXtasy Books Inc

Look for us online at:
www.eXtasybooks.com or www.devinedestinies.com

The Apprentice's Incubus

By

Diana Waters

DEDICATION

To Dante, who was by my side through much of this writing.
Rest in peace, my friend.

Chapter One

When Finn first heard the tell-tale sounds of a scuffle nearby, he ignored them. You didn't just go poking your nose into every disagreement that broke out nearby, or you'd likely only get your own fingers or nose broken for the effort—if you were lucky, that was.

A shout echoing down the alleyway—more of alarm than anger, Finn thought—made him reconsider. It wasn't kindness or even pity, but rather that the voice sounded out of place—not the kind of yell you usually heard when boys were scrapping among themselves over coin or food, or even when grown men were brawling. Besides, anything new that happened was always cause for curiosity. Sometimes you could profit if you were the first to know something—tidbits of information could be traded for favors, or an unexpected situation could turn into a sudden piece of luck. If it was a scuffle involving several people, all too busy trading blows to pay attention to one more small, bedraggled figure on the scene, you might even pick up a stray copper or scrap of bread. Finn was not strong, but he was quick on his feet, and that had proven useful in the past more times than he could count.

Edging his way warily closer to the commotion, the interconnecting alleyways were familiar enough to him that he felt in no real danger yet. Finn eventually found his way to four older boys, all about as scruffy as himself, dancing around a very tall but clearly not street-sharp stranger, who turned this way and that in the filthy alley as he tried to fend off their blows.

1

The boys were canny and darted around the older man, scurrying out of reach whenever he tried to make a grab for one of them, then skipping back in with a well-aimed kick or punch. They were too small to do any real damage, but together they were gradually wearing the man down, jumping up to scratch at his face, forcing him to work hard to defend himself.

There seemed little to gain from joining the fray, and Finn wouldn't have interfered had he not seen one of the boys was Jasom, the largest of the gang, laughter painted plain on his face as he jeered at the stranger, raking at the man's eyes with his fingernails.

"Can't see us? Can't fight us. Give it up, come on, we know you've got it, it's ours by right now—"

They were not aiming to kill, that much was clear, but Finn had a score to settle with Jasom. One night last winter, Jasom and his boys had stolen Finn's only blanket, leaving him to shiver in the snow. He'd only lived to tell the tale because some other poor soul down by the docks had taken pity and let him shelter under the same doorway for the night, their shaking bodies pressed together for security and warmth. Finn had not forgotten. In this city, sooner or later, a debt was always repaid.

Even so, he was not fool enough to get involved in a fight there was no way he'd win. He left plenty of space between him and the gang of boys as he yelled to get their attention, drawing it away from the hapless stranger for a moment. "Hey! *Hey!* Back off, I'm calling the City Watch!"

Jasom jerked to a stop and whirled around to face him. His sneer did not falter when he recognized the speaker. "Fuck off, Finny. You wouldn't dare—"

Finn sucked in a breath. "Over here! *Help!* Murder, *murder*, help us, gods, he's got a knife—" He belted out the words at the top of his lungs, adding in a high-pitched shriek for good measure, praying there actually was someone from the Watch close enough to hear.

Anyone with half a brain did their best to steer clear of the Watch, and Jasom's expression grew even uglier, if such a thing was possible. "You'll shut your mouth, damn you, or I'll kick your bloody teeth in—"

Finn grinned and let out another wailing cry, even louder and more dramatic than the last, his throat raw with it, and to his gratification, heard an answering shout from somewhere in the distance.

Maybe it was the Watch, maybe it wasn't, but even Jasom wasn't foolhardy enough to chance it. Even if his gang had possessed a single weapon between them other than their fists, no gaggle of boys would win against a single member of the Watch—and the soldiers never patrolled alone. More to the point, the Watch both wore and carried steel, and unlike most of the street urchins roaming the alleyways or skirting the edges of Market Square, would probably be applauded if they just so happened to kill someone in a fight. After all, it wasn't murder if you lived on the *other* side of the bridge.

"I'll be back for you, little Finny, don't think I won't." The words were spat into his face as the gang of boys melted away, back into the safety of the twisting passages. A few other choice words heralded their flight.

Finn was left with the overly tall stranger, both of them breathing heavily. Finn took another careful two steps back, just in case the man was more dangerous than he appeared, although he somehow doubted it. The man might have been large, but he also seemed confused, peering vaguely around him as though he was unsure what had just happened.

"Excuse me. Have you seen my eyeglasses? They should be on the ground around here somewhere . . ."

Finn blinked, instinctively casting about for the item. He saw them almost at once, lying several feet away from where they'd been knocked from the man's face at some point during the scuffle.

"They're broken." He picked them up and handed them over cautiously, still keeping an arm's length between himself and the stranger.

"My thanks." The man put them on, and although they now sat crookedly on his nose, one of the circles of glass showing spidery cracks where it had partially shattered, he seemed genuinely grateful. "Ah. So *you're* my savior, are you?"

"I s'pose. Here. You dropped this too." This time Finn allowed himself to get closer, sensing the man posed no threat. He handed over a silver piece that had rolled along the ground.

The man held the coin up to his face, rubbing the dust away and examining it, then looking back down at Finn, taking his measure. "This would have paid for a handsome meal," he said slowly. "Several handsome meals, in fact."

Finn shrugged. "It's yours. I can take care of myself just fine."

"Yes, I can see that. Well." The man appeared to be thinking. "Can I perhaps offer *you* a meal then? I owe you at least that much. Besides, I have a proposition for you."

Finn immediately edged away again, his eyes narrowing. "What kind of proposition?" He was no fool. That was the way people talked who wanted things out of you. Bad things, usually — things that hurt.

Noticing his suspicion, the man held up his hands, showing that he hid nothing. "A job. Nothing more. If you don't want it, you can go on your way and I'll not stop you. And either way, I'll still pay for the meal — whatever you want. I have enough here — " He paused, digging around in his pocket for the leather purse that the gang of boys from earlier had not quite managed to take. His hand came away empty.

"Do you happen to know — ah." The man's gaze sharpened.

Finn offered a smile, not totally devoid of sympathy, but not ashamed either. "Sorry." You did what you had to, even if that sometimes meant being a bastard.

"Sorry enough to give it back? Please, it's nearly all I have for the moment. Once I've completed this week's orders . . ."

The man's voice was steady, neither angry nor even pleading, and for that, Finn took a moment to consider. He hadn't had time to look yet, but the purse felt heavy, plenty of coins weighing it down. Even if they were all copper, it would still be enough to keep him fed, warm and dry for at least a couple of weeks — probably far longer, if he was careful.

On the other hand, he was undeniably curious. This stranger clearly meant him no harm — what job might he be talking about, and what might that eventually lead to? There could be great advantage in thinking beyond mere survival in the short term, and besides, he was hungry enough that a good meal — a *real* meal, with meat and wheaten bread instead of rye or barley, in the kind of place where you could sit down and not worry about someone assaulting you or trying to steal your food — was tempting. No respectable tavern would usually allow someone like Finn through its doors, even if he'd had the money to pay for the privilege.

Into the silence came a long, low growl. Finn looked down at his stomach, then back up at the man. He tossed the purse through the air and the man caught it neatly, looking a little surprised.

"Thank you," he said. "You pick the place. Wherever you like. I'll follow your lead."

Finn hesitated. "Any decent place'll kick me out when they see me."

"They won't when you're with me. I'll show them the color of my coin beforehand, if I must."

Finn nodded. Too late to change his mind now — it was take

the meal or nothing. Still wondering if he'd made the wrong decision in giving back the purse so easily, he led the way out of the alley and back onto the cobbled streets, keeping a ready eye out for trouble as he followed his nose to a nearby tavern.

Finn chose the Dancing Hart—partly because of the large trestle tables that would leave a good amount of space between anyone seated on the opposite side, partly because the stranger would hardly be able to try anything in such a public establishment, but mostly for the temptingly rich aroma of simmering meat emanating from within.

One of the workers, a sturdy and big-bosomed woman wiping down one of the tables near the door, shot Finn a dirty look, then continued staring at him pointedly. Then she caught sight of the man accompanying him who, despite the mussed hair, broken eyeglasses and numerous scratches about his face, was clearly used to being treated with more respect. He gave her a polite nod and strode past, and seeing they were dining together, she let them be.

"Ale," said the man when another woman, this one younger and more friendly-looking, came up to ask after their pleasure. "And water for the boy. What hot food is there available in the kitchen?"

"Beef and potato pie. We've got fresh bread, too, if you want, sir. Or we've a nice stew, hearty like."

The man shot Finn a questioning glance. "Whatever you like."

Finn was torn, and the man gave a quiet laugh, though not mocking. "Could you do us each a bit of both?" he asked, smiling at the serving woman. "It's been a very long morning."

"Aye." The woman dimpled and scurried away.

Left in relative privacy, the man extended an open hand toward Finn. "I'm Kestrall. Again, I thank you for your earlier assistance."

"Finn. Thanks for the food." The odors coming from the kitchen made his stomach whine again, this time high-pitched and pleading, but Kestrall did not make comment, even after the serving woman came back with their food and Finn began shoveling it in his mouth without bothering to speak another word.

It had been a long time since Finn had tasted hot food, let alone something so substantial. He forced himself to slow down eventually, aware he would throw it up later if he ate too quickly now, which would have been an unforgivable waste. Finally, he looked up and wiped his mouth. Kestrall was eying him, though his expression was not one of distaste, merely curiosity, and perhaps a hint of pity.

"How old are you, Finn?"

Finn shrugged. "Dunno." His age had never mattered — either you were strong enough to be of use or old enough to use your body, or you weren't, and that was all people mostly cared about.

"Do you have any parents? Relatives?"

"Dunno."

Kestrall kept his patience. "Well, do you remember having any?"

"Ma was a whore," Finn said baldly. "I remember her, a bit. She's gone now. Don't know where. Pa could've been any one of a hundred. More, maybe."

"So where do you live?"

Finn gave another shrug. There seemed no point in lying, or even in gentling the truth. "Around. I got kicked out of the whorehouse when I got too big. I sleep near the docks sometimes, or there's hidden places this side of the river where the rooftops meet. You can usually shelter from the rain there. Warm your back against a chimney for a while, if you're lucky. Or smart." He wasn't bragging. Stupid people died quickly, and Finn wasn't stupid.

"I see." Kestrall looked thoughtful. "And do you ever do odd jobs for people? Fetching, carrying, things of that nature?"

"Sometimes. I'm too small to get work by the docks mostly, but I help load wagons there when there's a need, or around Market Square. I've scrubbed hearths, carted water or washing, run messages . . ." Finn continued to chew what was left in his bowl, enjoying the flavor of the stew more now that the initial wave of hunger had passed. Hopefully it wouldn't be too rich for his stomach.

"You're not apprenticed to anyone, then?"

"Nah. Else I wouldn't be living on the street, would I?"

"Hm." Kestrall ran a hand over his neatly trimmed beard.

"You said you had a *proposition*." Finn leaned on the word, putting down his spoon and resting his elbows on the table pointedly.

"Aye, I do." Kestrall pushed up his eyeglasses, speaking more purposefully now. "I'm in need of a likely lad, not too young. Someone who can stay in my home and help me out when I've a need."

"Help out with what, exactly?" Finn didn't think Kestrall was any kind of threat—at least, he didn't look violent, or like he wanted to tup anyone unawares—but you could never be too careful. Even the priests sometimes tried to tempt a boy or girl with offers of food scraps, only to take advantage in the worst of ways as soon as they let their guard down. Finn had heard plenty of tales and was not eager to find out firsthand if they were true.

"Nothing sordid, I assure you." Kestrall sighed. "I understand you may not yet trust me, but I'm no abuser of children. I won't lay a finger on you—nor let anyone else lay a finger on you—in either anger or unholy lust. At worst, the work I'm speaking of is purely tedious in nature. What I'm looking for is someone to run my errands for me — fetch ingredients from shops when I've need of them, or buy food when there's none to be found in the house. A bit of cleaning when called for, sweeping and the like. That's it."

"You don't have a manservant, or a woman, to do that already?"

Kestrall shook his head. "Not now. The last serving girl left for a bigger, more prosperous household. Not that I can blame her. I warned her before she took the job, but still, she got frightened off."

Finn rose an eyebrow.

"Again, not because of whatever you're thinking. I'm a magician," Kestrall stated matter-of-factly. "Not a very famous one, but competent enough. I'm not nobility and I don't work for rich folk. Sailors looking for protective charms when they're at sea and other such traveling folk. Young women wanting to attract their sweethearts. Mothers seeking to look out for their bairns or ward off sickness in the household. The odd businessman seeking luck for a new venture. I tinker on my own when I've time . . . there may have been a few, uh, explosions. Small ones," he hastily added when Finn rose his other eyebrow to join the first. "The point is, I need someone to take care of things around the place when I'm busy with my work. Most importantly, I need someone who's trustworthy and willing to learn, and who won't scare off easily. In exchange, I can offer a room — a *private* one," he emphasized, "that I'll make sure you can lock from the inside if you so choose, and enough to eat every day. Plus a few coppers a week for you to do with as you like." Kestrall settled back in his chair, raising his tankard to his mouth and giving Finn some time to think.

It did not take Finn long. He'd been taking stock of Kestrall as the man had been talking, noticing the frayed cuffs on his shirt, the smudges here and there about his clothing. His hands were calloused but mostly clean, his beard short and neat. His boots were filthy, but Finn, who had never worn shoes himself, could hardly blame him for that, and his face was open, easy to read. Kestrall was either the best liar in the world or he was exactly as he said — a respectable house magician of no great means, in the market for a house servant who wouldn't jump at loud noises. It was no difficult choice to make — although just to be safe, he asked one more question.

"Why were you in that alleyway?"

Kestrall looked faintly embarrassed. "If you must know . . . one of the boys you helped run off grabbed me by the arm as I was walking by. He said one of his friends was injured, begged me to help — it didn't even cross my mind it could be a ploy to relieve me of my purse. I followed where he led without a second thought."

Finn snorted. That was one of the oldest tricks in the book, and no man or woman with any kind of street smarts would have fallen for it. Kestrall was clearly too unsuspecting and too kind for his own good — and Finn couldn't remember the last time he'd met anyone like that.

"All right," said Finn simply. "I'll work for you."

"Good." Kestrall adjusted his still-lopsided eyeglasses again. "I don't suppose you can read?" he asked hopefully.

"A bit."

Kestrall looked at him.

Finn shuffled a little in his seat. "Not really."

"Never mind. You seem a bright enough lad. I'll find some time to teach you."

Finn let out a breath. He smiled — his first real smile since they'd met. "Good." He picked up a slice of pie, the crust crumbling away in his mouth, warm and comforting. "Thank you."

Kestrall was as good as his word. His home was spacious enough, if somewhat cluttered and chaotic, and lay in a perfectly respectable part of town, still this side of the river. To Finn, it seemed like a mansion at first, though it was clear that Kestrall thought it merely serviceable. His neighbors were clerks and craftsmen, tutors and fellow shop owners, and their children, dressed in well-patched but practical clothes and sturdy shoes, played together in the streets without violence. If there were any brawls, they took place elsewhere, and if anyone drank to excess or indulged in other, more dangerous substances, they had the decency to do so in private.

The first couple of days, Kestrall did not demand Finn do any work at all, despite Finn making it clear he was willing, and to work hard at that. Instead, he was shown around the house and told more about what he might expect to do — and sometimes see or hear — in the course of his duties.

"Nothing I do up here will be a danger to you," Kestrall promised him. "All my experiments are conducted downstairs in the basement, surrounded only by earth and stone. No book or object that's able to do you harm is kept upstairs. So long as you don't venture downstairs alone, all is perfectly safe."

Finn could not keep the burning curiosity from his face, and Kestrall laughed and showed him the basement. To Finn's disappointment, there was little to be seen beyond a large wooden table — this scarred and pitted with numerous ink stains and burn marks from candles — rows of old and tattered books, glass jars filled with dried herbs and other such ingredients, and stacks of parchment and writing materials scattered haphazardly around. It was a perfectly ordinary-looking, if again rather messy sort of room, and upon seeing it for himself, Finn felt little inclination to meddle.

His own chamber was small but not uncomfortable. Indeed, Finn had not slept in a real bed in years, and this one had a pillow and not one but two blankets, both for him. The door, Kestrall promised, would be altered so Finn could bolt it from within if he wished, and though there was no window, sunlight filtered in from the hallway leading to the kitchen if the door was left open. This, Kestrall explained, doubled as the upstairs workplace, where customers were also allowed to come in and wait for their orders to be finished if they so desired. Finn's chamber also contained a small chest of drawers, empty once Kestrall cleared out what he called a pointless collection of knickknacks, and a wooden shelf lining the wall, with yet more dusty books that Kestrall likewise cleared away for him.

Finn was supplied with another set of clothes the very next day. They were not new, but they fit and were comfortable, and came into his hands far cleaner than anything Finn remembered owning even as a child. Before he was allowed to put any of them on, however, Kestrall made Finn bathe. There was a tiny, enclosed courtyard behind the house that Kestrall claimed never saw much use, and there he paid a washerwoman to fill a large wooden tub with water. This took several trips, even with multiple people carting the water, which was lukewarm by the time the tub had been filled.

To Finn, it was a strange experience indeed. He kept himself as clean as he might, but this was no mean feat when the river was freezing even in the summer and the water there none too clean anyway. Kestrall disappeared back into the house, closing the door pointedly behind him, and Finn looked around warily. The courtyard walls were high — nobody would see him, or probably even hear him splashing about. After another long look in every direction, he stripped quickly and submerged himself, scrubbing his body with the cake of lye soap Kestrall had left for him. By the time Finn had finished, and his hair too had received a vigorous wash, the soap had all but disappeared entirely and the water had turned the color of mud. The clothes felt strange against his skin when Finn put them on afterward, and he ran his fingers through hair that felt oddly light.

Kestrall gave a whistle of amazement when he saw him. "Could've sworn your hair was a dark brown," he said.

"Why? What color is it?"

"Don't you know?"

Finn shook his head. He couldn't recall ever getting a good look at his own reflection. Kestrall fetched a small hand mirror, and Finn stared, angling his head and running his fingers through his hair again. It was brown, to be sure, but a light, warmish color with a few strands that, when the sun hit them, could almost be called golden.

"I can cut it short, or you can tie it back in a tail like mine if you prefer. You can decide later what you'd like best. For now . . ." Kestrall held out a thin band of leather.

Finn handed the mirror back. He took the piece of leather, glaring up at Kestrall to hide the rush of gratitude that suddenly threatened to overwhelm him.

"I think it's time I got to work now."

CHAPTER TWO

"Master Kestrall!" Finn walked out of the kitchen and peered down the stone steps leading to the basement. The door stood open, which meant Kestrall didn't mind any interruptions.

"What is it?" came the answering call.

"Rosie's at the door!" he shouted back, not bothering to walk all the way down.

"Who?"

"*Rosie*! The girl whose ma you've been making healing charms for!"

"Ah . . . yes. Of course. Tell her I'll be right up!"

Finn rolled his eyes and went back out into the kitchen. "He'll be right up, he says."

"Thanks, Finn." Rosie stirred her tea unconcernedly, glancing around at the mess.

It would have been messier still if Finn had not been there to keep things under precarious control. Kestrall was forever putting things down and promptly forgetting where they were only moments later, or buying so-called useful or one-of-a-kind items and then leaving them on the table and benches, where they accumulated until Finn made a point of making Kestrall do something about them—this usually being to cram them into already overflowing drawers or onto cluttered shelves. Then there were the books and old manuscripts, the house constantly full of these more than anything else. Some were only half-legible, old or faded with time and wear, and some were written in different languages. Kestrall's eyes lit up whenever he saw them in bookstores or pawnbrokers, and when he was too busy with customers or too tired to walk anywhere, having spent days locked up in the basement obsessing over arcane spells or rituals that seldom bore any result that Finn knew of, he would send Finn away to scour the shops on his behalf. It seemed Kestrall read about and dabbled in anything and everything—history, philosophy, herbology, alchemy, astronomy. Some days, he probably would not have eaten at all were it not for Finn, who had become well-used to his master's habits over the years.

"Sorry. I haven't cleaned yet today. Master Kestrall sent me to the apothecary for supplies. I guess he forgot about your appointment." Finn gave another internal sigh. If he hadn't come back when he had, Rosie would no doubt still be waiting on the doorstep while Kestrall was lost in his work, blind and deaf to the world around him.

"Nah, I don't mind. Besides, gets me out of the house. Ma's crankier than usual with her back. And I get to see you." Rosie sipped her tea, the cup hiding her mouth but her eyes staring at him boldly.

Finn looked away, uncomfortable, and was glad to hear his master's boots coming up the stairs.

"Young Rosie! You're lucky Finn reminded me you were coming yesterday, else your charm wouldn't be ready yet. I crafted it last night . . . er, Finn? You wouldn't happen to know..?"

Finn gave a long-suffering sigh and reached behind the tottering stack of books on the shelf behind where his master stood. "You put it here. For safekeeping, you said."

"So I did, there's a good lad. Here you are then, Rosie."

"Thank you, sir." Rosie dropped her gaze. "Ma's . . . she's been getting worse lately, so she says. Some days she can't even get out of bed."

"Hmm. Has the physicker been around?"

15

Rosie shook her head. "Says she trusts you more than whatever the physicker made her drink last time. Said it tasted of fish and piss."

"Rosie." Kestrall looked at her, and his voice was firm. "I've told your mother this before. These charms only aid in *recovery*. If she wants to be well, she must follow proper medical advice. I'm no physicker, and this charm will do nothing for the pain. Neither will any of the herbal infusions I brew. They serve only to relax the body. I don't make medicines, and I'll not sell what I have no mastery over."

"Yes, sir," Rosie whispered, and Kestrall relented.

"Come back next week," he said more gently. "I can try something a bit stronger with the herbs. But she *must* obey the physicker," he added.

"Aye. I'll tell her you said so." Rosie was all smiles again, and she glanced at Finn, mouth quirking up suggestively, before she took her leave, the woven charm clutched in her hand.

The door squealed closed behind her. Finn stood up and began clearing away the items on the table as best he could. A small spider scuttled past as he moved a sheaf of parchment.

"You could do worse than Rosie, you know." Kestrall stroked his beard thoughtfully.

Finn sputtered. "I've no interest in Rosie!"

"Well, she clearly has an interest in *you*," Kestrall pointed out.

"I'm too busy." Finn scowled. This was true enough, at least in part. He'd known children with more sense than Kestrall once the magician got lost in his work, not eating, not sleeping. The other part of that truth was that he was far more interested in catching the attention of someone else.

Jonti was the apprentice bookkeeper at the Crow's Nest, one of the shops Finn often frequented on Kestrall's behalf. Around twenty years of age and likely only slightly older than Finn, Jonti had broad shoulders, a strong, brown face and a smattering of freckles across his nose — and for months now, Finn had been trying to work up the courage to show his interest, thus far with resounding failure.

"Well, maybe you should make some time," suggested Kestrall. "She's a good lass and she enjoys your company. She's probably lonely now that she's taken charge of the market stand and doesn't have her mother to boss her around as much."

"Can we please talk about something else? Like the fact you've got enough useless stuff lying here to open a pawn shop of your own? If you're not going to do something about all this, you should just get rid of it. Especially the books," he added as Kestrall gaped. "You can't possibly read all of them, even if you never worked another day in your life."

"I will do no such thing!" Kestrall gathered up his books protectively, indignant. "These would have been destroyed without me. Such a waste of knowledge. Who knows if it's been recorded anywhere else?"

"They would've been destroyed because they're old and falling to bits," Finn pointed out.

"That doesn't mean they're not worth saving," Kestrall protested. "What long-forgotten pearls of wisdom might be hidden within these very pages?" He stroked the books lovingly.

"Maybe *I'm* not the one who should be making time for female company," said Finn pointedly. "When was the last time *you* went out?"

Kestrall cleared his throat and looked around, quickly changing the subject. "Did you get the herbs I asked for?"

"And some you didn't — you were nearly out of yarrow. Henbane, too."

"Oh, was I?" Kestrall was already busy flicking through one of the precious books he held in his arms. "Thank you,

Finn. Whatever would I do without you?"

Finn muttered to himself as he strode toward Market Square and the Crow's Nest, the spring winds still brisk on his face and hands. Two days — *two* days — and now his master was sending him back to purchase yet more books. At least Kestrall had made a list for the master bookkeeper in advance this time, and made sure Finn had enough money jangling in his pocket to purchase everything on it . . . and more, if he just happened to find something new or unusual, Kestrall had wheedled. Never mind that Finn would be the one to carry them all home. Never mind that they were rapidly running out of space to store the books they already had. He wasn't even convinced his master knew what half of them were. For his part, Finn still only read very slowly, but surely even the most well-educated man couldn't possibly read as many books as Kestrall now had in his entire lifetime?

The one bright side was that he would probably see Jonti, who worked alongside the master bookkeeper at the Crow's Nest nearly every day. Sometimes Finn only caught tantalizing glimpses of Jonti in the back room behind the counter, where he helped to flick through the books for damage, clean them, and sort them into neat piles depending on where in the shop they belonged. At other times, Finn was actually able to talk to him — if he could force a sensible sentence from his own mouth, anyway. Around the bookkeeper's apprentice, Finn grew awkward and tongue-tied, like he was still just a street brat who might earn a thrashing if he said the wrong thing.

Even so, Finn looked forward to seeing Jonti. He was bright and cheerful, and probably smart too, if he was a bookkeeper's apprentice, Finn reckoned. He was also tall — far taller than Finn — but then, Finn himself was only so small and skinny because he hadn't had enough food to make him grow when he was younger, according to Kestrall, and now no matter how much he ate, he never grew any taller. Finn didn't usually care what he looked like, but it was different when he was around Jonti, and so today his hair was neatly brushed, his face and hands free of dust from cleaning, his clothes freshly laundered.

Finn passed the candle maker, the pawnbroker and the tailor, doing his best to ignore the dark-robed figure who glared at him from the other side of the street as they passed one another. If it had taken him weeks to get used to sleeping in a bed in an enclosed room, it had taken months to get used to seeing such figures of authority walking the streets without promptly bolting in the other direction. Finn was no longer a street urchin who needed to fear priests or the Watch, and he certainly no longer looked it, but old habits were hard to quash—and why did priests always look so ill-tempered, anyway?

The priest turned a corner, but Finn quickened his pace anyway, until finally the familiar sound of the bell rang over his head as he entered the book shop, setting his stomach fluttering in an entirely different way.

"Coming!" The master bookkeeper bustled in from the back room. "Finn! Well, well. I'd barely finished sourcing what your master asked me for last time." He was a large man, like Kestrall, but barrel-chested and much rounder in the stomach, and with a wiry, bristling beard that jumped around as he spoke.

"I know." Finn sighed, digging the list out of his pocket. He knew it by heart because Kestrall had made him write each title down, claiming it was good practice. "Seven books in total, aye?"

The master bookkeeper nodded. "And not all easy to find, let me tell you. Wait a moment while I fetch them from out back."

Finn glanced about. "Is—er—Jonti in?"

"Aye, you'll find him around the corner. Mind the ladder."

His words made sense when Finn peered to the left. Jonti was balanced precariously on one of the top rungs of a ladder as he placed several books on an upper shelf. He didn't notice he had company, but still Finn felt his palms begin to sweat and the fluttering in his stomach making its way up into his throat. He wiped his hands surreptitiously on his trousers.

One of the books in Jonti's arms must have been off-balance, for just then, it slipped from its stack and fell to the floor. Jonti let out a quiet oath, thumping the rest of his pile down on the edge of the shelf and turning around to look. He broke into a smile when he noticed Finn. "Hey, it's the magician's apprentice, back again for another load of books!"

Finn tried to smile normally in return, but the expression felt wooden on his face. "Hi."

"Do us a favor, pick that up for me, would you?"

"Sure." Finn reached down and grasped the book. It was old and bound in leather that had probably once been quite handsome, although now it was scuffed and peeling, and he could only read half of the cover, the rest written in an unfamiliar language. "What's this?"

"Oh, some old spellbook or other. Leastwise, it claims to be. I can't make out even half of what's written in there though, and neither could my master even. Besides, some of the pages are so brittle they'll tear at any moment. Doubt it'll go for much."

"Oh." Finn handed the book back, watching longingly as Jonti headed back up the ladder.

"I heard Rosie was back to see your master again."

Finn made an unintelligible noise at the back of his throat. Jonti was taking an interest in what was going on at Finn's home? No, no, he was just curious about Kestrall—everyone always wanted to know what a magician got up to, even though Finn could have told them it was just as exciting as working in a book shop was to Jonti. They might call Finn the magician's apprentice, but in reality, his job mostly involved cleaning and running errands. There hadn't even been an explosion down in the basement for weeks now.

"She says her ma's gotten worse again, but that she swears by your master's charms," Jonti continued. "Say, think he could make one for me?"

Finn shrugged. "Maybe." He cleared his throat. "What kind of charm?"

Jonti's gaze met his from where he was still balanced on top of the ladder, one strong arm braced on the shelf for support. "A love charm," he said, and his blue eyes sparkled so wonderfully that Finn made an almost audible gasp.

"L-love . . ."

"Charm," Jonti finished, grinning. "Well? Think he'll do it for me if you asked him?"

"*Me?*" Finn heard his voice squeak and cleared his throat.

"Well, yeah. You're the apprentice. Maybe you could even make it yourself, if your master's busy."

Finn swallowed and then choked on his own saliva. "Uh, I, suppose if, maybe—"

"Only, I don't have much money at the moment. 'Course, I could pay you back soon enough. So, what do you think?"

Finn couldn't think at all, feverish imaginings crowding into his mind. Jonti wanted a love charm for someone. Jonti was staring at him, asking him for this favor, smiling in that way that made his eyes light up. Jonti was asking *him*, the apprentice, for a love charm, despite everyone knowing that Kestrall was a soft touch who regularly allowed his customers to pay later if they needed something now that they couldn't afford.

"I'll . . ." The word came out too soft to be heard, and Finn cleared his throat again and shuffled his feet. "I'll see what I can do."

"Good." Jonti grinned again, his teeth white against the beautiful brown of his face. "Thanks, Finn."

"Finn!" The friendly booming voice of the master bookkeeper made him jump. "I have your order ready."

"Oh! Yes, sir."

He followed the bookkeeper back to the desk, where the older man listed out the titles one by one. Finn was barely listening, all too aware of Jonti, who had followed him to the desk, standing nearby. " . . . And *Blessed Gatherings: Herbs to be Gathered Under the New Moon*," the bookkeeper finished.

"Yes. Right. Thanks." Finn fumbled with his coin purse, dumped half of the coins on the floor by mistake, and scurried to pick them up, his face and neck burning. "Sorry."

As Jonti helped him gather up the coins before they could roll too far, their hands brushed. Finn jumped.

"Here."

"Thanks. Sorry," said Finn again, helplessly. Gods, what would someone like Jonti want with the likes of Finn? More importantly, what would the likes of Finn do with someone like Jonti, once he'd . . . once they'd . . . Finn shook his head, trying to rid it of the images that stuck there, repeating over and over like a scene from a play. Jonti, long-limbed and naked, in Finn's bed, his bare chest gleaming gold in the candlelight, the shadows dancing over his skin. Jonti's hands on him, over him, gripping Finn's shoulders and stroking down, down . . .

"Say, you've got too much here, even this lot's not worth all that."

"What?"

"Jonti's right, lad. Your master has plenty here."

It took Finn a moment to catch up to the present. He shrugged. "He said it was all to go to you. Or other books."

"Here, take this one too, then. Maybe it's rare enough he'll like it." Jonti was still holding the old leather-bound book in his hands that had fallen earlier. "Master?"

The master bookkeeper examined the tome, his hands turning the pages gingerly. "I don't see why not. I'll likely have trouble selling such a thing myself. Repairing the damage would be costly, and there's at least four different languages written here."

"Thanks."

Jonti helped to pile the books into his arms. "Sure you can make it back home with all that? Maybe I should walk with you to help . . ."

"Jonti! No skiving off work, boy, don't think I don't know what you're up to."

"Whoops." Jonti grinned. "Caught out."

The mere thought of Jonti wanting to accompany him home, the two of them walking shoulder to shoulder through the busy market square, was enough to send Finn scuttling from the shop in a state of half-aroused mortification.

Kestrall was in the kitchen when Finn returned. He turned to award Finn for his efforts with a sheepish smile. "There's a good lad. Put them down here."

He had cleared enough room for the new books, at least. Huffing from the effort of lugging them all the way back from the book shop, Finn gratefully shoved them onto the table, where they immediately tumbled from their neat pile. He rolled his shoulders, stretching them, while his master looked eagerly through his newest acquisitions.

"Ah! Yes, excellent. Not in as bad condition as I thought this one would be either, for all its age. Second edition, mind. Still, an excellent tome. And this one—a good reference book for amulets made only from clay. A must-have for any magician's library . . . I wonder what could have happened to my older copy?"

"Buried under a hundred other books, no doubt," Finn groused.

"Well, if I ever find it, it always pays to have a spare . . . and what's this?"

Finn picked up the leather-bound book. "Oh, this one the master bookkeeper gave me for free. Said the money you gave was too much, and this one might be rare." He squinted at the cover. "Dunno what language the top part is written in, but the bottom half says . . . *Magicks*—it's pretty faded—*of the Earth* . . . something something . . . *Unlawful Carnal*—"

Kestrall choked and snatched the book from his hands, staring at the cover. Fingers trembling, he cracked it open and turned the first page, staring down at the words speechlessly.

"What is it? Is it that rare?"

"It's . . . this isn't something I ever thought . . ."

"What?" said Finn again, curious. He angled his head, trying to get a better look, and Kestrall glanced up at him, snapping the book shut again, still wide-eyed and now breathing a little heavily.

"Finn. You're not to touch this book, understand? It's . . . it's not *safe*, not for an apprentice."

"Why not?"

"Because . . . it's just not, that's all. It contains magicks that aren't suitable for . . . for . . . most people. There are spells here that, if performed incorrectly or . . ." Kestrall swallowed. "Or at all. They could do very serious things that even a well-trained magician might not be able to undo."

Kestrall had spoken quickly, almost urgently, tripping over his words, and Finn frowned. "It's not as though I could read it anyway—"

"Nonetheless. I will keep this book downstairs."

Finn huffed, even more curious now but not about to argue. "Fine. And what about all these?" He waved at the mess now scattered across the table.

"Oh . . ." Oddly, Kestrall looked as though he'd completely forgotten about the books he'd been exclaiming over just a moment ago. "I'll take care of those later. We've no more appointments today, aye? You can have the rest of the day off if you like . . . I'll be busy."

"Right." Finn was about to ask about the love charm Jonti had mentioned but decided he'd do it later, when his master was less distracted. If he did so now, Kestrall would forget in five minutes — Finn knew that obsessive gleam in his master's eyes all too well.

"And Finn?"

"Master Kestrall?" Finn turned from where he'd been rummaging through the cupboards, hungry and looking for the leftover bread.

"I'll probably be downstairs much of the evening as well. If anyone comes to the door, I'm not to be disturbed. Not for anyone — is that clear?"

"Fine, I got it."

The instruction was common enough — Kestrall often spent whole nights without sleep, tinkering with rare ingredients or sudden unconventional ideas, driven by newfound spells and ancient knowledge.

Still, Finn thought as his master all but tripped in his haste to get down the stairs, then pushed the basement door closed behind him, the book still pressed close to his chest — still, if Kestrall thought Finn didn't know it was something in that book that had so excited him, and that Finn wouldn't take a closer look for himself as soon as the coast was clear, then Kestrall was a fool.

CHAPTER THREE

Once he'd eaten a late lunch, the matter of the book put aside for the moment in favor of settling his rumbling stomach, Finn decided he would try making the love charm for Jonti himself, just as Jonti had suggested.

Well, and why not, Finn thought to himself, rolling up his sleeves. The charm contained no ingredients that were dangerous or forbidden to him, and Kestrall had always told him that most charms were more effective when created by one of the people it was supposed to affect—it was why Kestrall made his own charms when he wanted something for himself rather than purchase them from another magician. Besides, Finn had watched Kestrall make hundreds of love charms over the years—these being one of their most popular items—so he wouldn't even need to consult a primer. Although his duties thus far had been mostly limited to that of an errand boy, this was admittedly because Finn had shown no great interest in making charms and tinctures himself, once the initial curiosity of living in a magician's house had passed. Even so, his master often invited Finn to watch as he went about his work, saying that every boy should have a trade, and that this might as well be Finn's if he didn't want to spend the rest of his life attending solely to the needs of others.

The herbs for the love charm were all in the kitchen. Crushed rosemary and violets were plentiful—Finn always made sure they never ran low in stock. To this he added vervain, dutifully collected during the new moon, and hawthorn. Mixing each of these together in a small wooden bowl in the amounts he had been shown, he then found the extract of lavender from the shelf behind him and added three careful drops, and finally two of jasmine. He mixed the ingredients together again, the dried herbs quickly soaking up the oils, as he muttered the simple incantation under his breath that would bind everything together in spirit as well as physical form. Intention in any charm was important, Kestrall had emphasized time and time again, and an incantation was designed not only to activate the ingredients, but also to focus the mind of the person creating the charm. Without this, it would simply be a jumble of all but meaningless objects.

"Spirits of love, hear me. Spirits of desire, gather near. In this spell I invoke thee, in light and in shadow, by sun and by starlight, from fire and from water. Seek ye out those two who wish to be joined in body and in soul."

Then Finn lit a small white candle, carefully spooned out the ingredients from the bowl, and emptied them into a roughly woven pouch, plain in color but stitched near the top in red. Taking a coarse piece of twine, he wrapped it around the top of the pouch to form a tight knot, sealing the ingredients safely inside. Finally he passed the pouch clockwise around the candle, muttering the same incantation thrice more.

It was done. Satisfied, Finn looked at his handiwork and slipped the pouch into his pocket. He would give it to Jonti in the morning and tell him not to worry about the payment. The ingredients were plentiful, and he knew Kestrall would not mind their use. Jonti need only place the amulet under his pillow before bed, think of the one he wished to be bound to—Finn shivered, already flushing again at the thought—and go to sleep. The charm would work its magick soon enough, albeit perhaps not in the way Jonti imagined.

"Charms such as these are not intended to make someone fall in love or even in lust against their will," Kestrall had told him firmly when Finn had asked, "but rather to embolden them to admit their desires to the one on their mind. We only refer to them as love charms because it's easier for people to understand that way. Still, they're powerful enough, so long as they be created with good intent."

Since Finn was already well aware of his attraction to Jonti, and Jonti had already shown his interest in Finn, the spell should work quickly, he mused. Probably it would only give Jonti the nudge he needed to speak his desires to Finn aloud, and then they could . . . well, they could . . .

"Gods." Finn buried his face in his hands, feeling the heat from it emanating through his palms. He really needed to focus on something else, otherwise he knew he would drive himself senseless.

Finn retired to bed early that night but could not sleep. He tossed and turned, fingering the love charm he had put under his own pillow for the time being for good luck. His nightshirt twisted uncomfortably around his body, and he was tormented by thoughts of Jonti. However, it was not the love charm itself on his mind, but what would happen after that.

The painful truth of the matter, Finn admitted to himself, was that he had absolutely no experience in matters of the body. Infatuation was one thing. You kept it to yourself and, if you had to, wrang yourself dry until the thoughts passed and you could focus again. It didn't matter if you'd never lain with anyone before — it was the body's natural instinct taking over, making you rub and pinch and stroke in all the right places until your seed was spilled and your body was your own again. You didn't need to think about anybody else, their desires, their wishes, and you didn't need to worry about what it might feel like to have someone else do things to you — how you would appear in their eyes, if it would hurt, if they would know exactly where and how to touch to make you feel good and not like you were just a warm body to rut against.

Finn was no stranger to sex. He'd been born in a whore-house, after all, and though too young at the time to know exactly what that entailed, he knew men paid women — and sometimes other men — to make them feel good. Later, out on the streets, he'd stumbled across people using one another's bodies in much the same way, sometimes for coin and some-times not. Women too old or too plain to find employment in a whorehouse, or whose minds were too addled with drink or other things, lured men into alleyways, where they fucked one another against the rough, cold stone walls. Street boys, once they'd gotten too old to pick pockets or did not look strong enough to find enough paid labor, sometimes did the same. Once in a while, Finn had seen people fucking just for the sake of it. If the other party was unwilling or even too far gone to protest, you averted your eyes and walked the other way just the same. It didn't do well to come between a man and his hunger, lest you get your teeth kicked in or become the bait yourself. This, Finn had managed to avoid through a combination of street smarts and, once or twice, pure, dumb luck.

As a result, he knew nothing of matters of the flesh where they concerned someone else. He had no idea what it was like to touch someone real and make them feel pleasure, and no notion of what it was like to be touched by anyone else in re-turn. If the sweethearts he saw holding hands sometimes in Market Square were any indication, love was indeed some-thing that brought pleasure, but in terms of physical desire, what little knowledge he had told him that it brought mostly pain, humiliation and squalidness. Perhaps that was why so many people on the streets and in whorehouses tended to have such a fondness for the bottle — to make them forget or to dull their senses while their bodies were used in such a way.

Finn sighed and turned over again, now on his back and the love charm clutched in his hand, staring up at the ceiling. He should never have made it for Jonti, he realized now. He'd gotten too far ahead of himself, letting excitement get the better of him. Clearly, Finn was not ready, and maybe he never would be. He would bring no pleasure to Jonti — he did not know how — and while Finn's body clearly worked as most other boys' did, he wasn't sure he wanted to find out what it was really like to give it up to another. The entire concept of sex to bring both parties pleasure was plainly something he'd missed out on, growing up on the streets, and now that he was not even really a boy any longer, he was probably too old to learn. He'd best get rid of the love charm and tell Jonti that his master was too busy to make one. Jonti would move on, maybe fall in love with someone who wasn't so utterly ignorant of bed sport and all that was supposed to come with it.

His mind made up, Finn pushed back the blankets. He would get rid of the love charm now, he decided — that way, at least his mind would be clearer, and he could finally sleep.

In the kitchen, he lit a new candle — for all charms had to be disposed of properly once they were no longer needed — and held the small pouch over the flame. His nose had only just caught a whiff of the fabric beginning to singe when suddenly, a hoarse cry rang out from the basement.

Finn jerked away from the candle, almost knocking it clean over, with a yelp of his own, quickly cut off as he realized his master had probably caused some kind of explosion again — his efforts at alchemy especially be damned. Even so, his heart continued to thump as, still clutching the love charm in one hand and the candle in the other, Finn made his way down the hall and to the top of the steps leading downward.

"Master Kestrall?" he called tentatively.

The basement door did not open, and Finn heard nothing

more for a moment. That was odd, since Kestrall, usually calm and composed, and unfailingly polite to everyone he spoke to, cursed like a sailor every time he'd spent hours upon hours on an experiment that failed in such dramatic fashion. Neither had Finn caught the sound of glass shattering — another very common occurrence — or the thump of books hitting the ground as they were knocked from their perches.

Oh gods, what if Kestrall had actually hurt himself this time? The explosions tended to be small, for all they were so loud, but maybe there had been some real damage — his master might be wounded, unconscious, or both.

"Master Kestrall?" Finn called again, this time a little louder. The door stayed firmly closed, and Kestrall had forbidden any interruption to his work, no matter the hour. Still, if his master was hurt and needed help, Finn would have no way of knowing. He could ease the door open, surely, and just peek inside to make sure his master was all right? Even if the door was barred from within, Finn could peer through the keyhole, and if he saw his master on the ground or caught sight of any blood, he could raise the alarm and gather enough neighbors to strong-arm the door.

These thoughts racing through his head, Finn made his way down the steps. He tried the door carefully, quietly, and finding it indeed locked, kneeled on the ground and pressed one eye to the keyhole.

And gaped, shocked into immobility, at the scene unfolding before him.

His master was bound and stripped, not a stitch of clothing to cover his nakedness. His wrists were tied together in front of him, and his hair lay unbound and disheveled. He was kneeling, his hands on the floor and his head down, so that it fell about his face, though Finn could see from the movement of his chest that he was breathing heavily, perhaps gasping. Parts of his back and his torso were reddened with what looked like burn marks, and his posture was tense, muscles straining as though he wanted to flee but could not.

In front of Kestrall stood a demon.

Finn knew it was a demon as soon as he saw it. He didn't know how, but still he knew, for all the demon had taken human form and was dressed in human clothing. Perhaps it was the eyes — a fierce, wild green that reflected the light from the candles around the chamber. Those eyes appeared to burn as well, almost as though they contained some kind of flame within them. Even the demon's hair was a bold, fiery red.

The demon looked down upon Finn's master and smiled. "Not too much too soon, I hope, my pretty pet magician?"

Kestrall's body gave a shudder, and he did not answer.

"For you are my pet, at least for the space of this night. You understand, of course? A magician should always understand what it is he wreaks." The demon took a step closer so that it loomed over Kestrall. Finn's master was large and powerfully built, both tall and broad of shoulder, but even so, the demon dwarfed him in size. "Well? Answer me, magician."

"Y-yes . . ."

"Good. Then you will also understand that I am nobody's *plaything*." With clenched fist, the demon jerked Kestrall's hair back so that the magician's throat was bared. Then it kneeled beside Kestrall, bringing its lips to the man's neck. "No, you are *my* plaything, and so I am marking you as a reminder."

Finn stared, afraid, transfixed, as Kestrall moaned at the touch.

"Don't forget it." The demon released Kestrall's head and stood. "I like you on your knees like this, pet." The demon seemed more amused than angry now. "It becomes you. I enjoy seeing strong men supplicant before me . . . and I see that you enjoy being humbled. You enjoy it very much, in fact." The demon licked his lips as though he could taste Kestrall's pain. "Now stand up, pet."

Kestrall moaned again and shook his head, trying to curl in on himself, shelter his body and his shame from sight, but the demon only smiled more widely. "Don't hide yourself from me. Embrace your indignity. *Revel* in it. Or must I really teach you to do so?"

With a muffled sob, Kestrall got awkwardly to his feet, though his hands struggled to preserve his modesty. "Please don't . . . don't make me . . ."

"Ah." The demon closed its gleaming eyes and shuddered in what looked like pleasure. "Your desire speaks more loudly than your words ever could, my pet. Keep speaking them if you like—they only serve to feed my hunger. But first . . ." One hand shot out to seize Kestrall's wrists in a punishing grip.

Finn's arms shook with the effort of holding still as he watched, the candle's flame wavering, shock making him cold and then suddenly hot and sweating again. His master had nowhere to hide now, nothing to disguise his obvious arousal, and his face was pleading, tortured.

"Please," Kestrall whispered again, and then closed his eyes as the demon stroked his face with his other hand. "*Please* . . ."

"Patience, patience. First, a lesson. Then, your reward."

"No!" Kestrall struggled, attempting to free himself, but the demon was clearly far stronger. It let go of Kestrall and watched almost lazily as the magician tried desperately to loosen the knots, the leather cutting into his wrists.

"As much as I enjoy watching the struggle, I think I would enjoy watching something else from you even more." The demon put one hand to Kestrall's chest and pushed, not hard, but Finn watched his master stumble backward even so, until his back was pressed against one of the bare stone walls of the chamber.

"Keep standing. If your hands or knees touch the floor again before I say they may, I will punish you dearly for it." The demon narrowed its eyes. "Understood?"

Dumbly, Kestrall nodded.

"I require a true answer from you, pet."

"Y-yes . . ."

"Excellent." The demon flicked its gaze downward. "Then touch yourself."

Kestrall's own eyes flared wide and panicked. "What?"

"Touch yourself. Give yourself pleasure. I will observe."

"But . . . but I—but you can't—"

"*Pet*," said the demon, a warning tone in its voice. "I can do whatever it is I like to you, and you *will* obey." The unspoken *or else* was clear.

Kestrall shook his head, but even as he did so, his hands moved haltingly to his groin. He hesitated, shot another agonized look at his captor, and began to stroke himself. The movements were slow and clumsy, his hands trying to move in ways that the ties around his wrists would not let him, and the demon smirked and flicked one of its fingers. At that, the ties seemed to loosen a little, and Kestrall trembled as his knees began to shake. He closed his eyes again.

"No, no," the demon clicked its tongue, grinning. "Your eyes stay on me. Also, when I say stop, you must do so immediately. If you do not . . . well . . ." The warning was once again unmistakable.

Finn's fingernails dug painfully into his palm. He wanted to scream, he wanted to run—but if he did, would he put his master in more danger? Might the demon be able to kill them both? His breath came in ragged gasps as he tried to keep silent, and he covered his mouth with his hand, the love charm lying forgotten, dropped on the floor by his knees. He continued to watch, heart pounding painfully, as Kestrall stood and stroked himself, wild-eyed and panting.

"Good . . . oh yes, very good indeed . . ." The demon breathed deeply, humming in appreciation, and stepped closer, his gaze roving Kestrall's body—and now Finn could see that what Kestrall was doing was also having an effect on the demon. With no sense of shame that Finn could discern, with no hesitation whatsoever, it jerked down its trousers to its thighs, exposing itself to Kestrall's gaze. "*Ah* . . ." Sighing in abandon, the demon too began to stroke, watching Kestrall do the same all the while, occasionally releasing a groan of undisguised pleasure. "Yes, pet, just like that . . . *yes* . . ."

Finn was beginning to feel faint from lack of air. Beads of sweat trickled down his neck. He was hard, he realized suddenly, painfully so, and he tried to hold back a guttural sound of his own as he palmed his arousal, vaguely aware of what he was doing but somehow unable to stop himself. It was like a dream, one in which he could not control his own body.

"Stop now," said the demon abruptly, and Kestrall's hands fell away, the light from the candles making the moisture on them glisten.

But the demon did not stop, and neither could Finn—he tried desperately to regain control as his breath emerged fast and ragged from his throat. Kestrall made a wounded sound, like an animal that had been whipped, as the demon continued to look at him, not faltering in his movements.

"Do you like what you see, pet?"

"Yes," Kestrall gasped. His body was trembling in earnest now.

"Do you desire this body, enough to sacrifice your own?"

"Yes, gods, please—"

"And would you like your own release?"

"Yes!"

"Then, for your honesty, you shall be rewarded."

The demon came closer still, until the two were near enough to touch—and this time, the demon dropped to *its* knees, and its mouth opened, and he took Kestrall's arousal inside of it.

Kestrall gave a cry that echoed around the chamber, the demon hummed again in pleasure, and Finn bit the hand covering his mouth so hard that his teeth punctured the skin. His body, too, jerked, so that his shoulders, which had been all but leaning on the door for support, thumped heavily against it.

The sound was not loud, but the demon's eyes snapped up, and though there was no way he should have been able to see Finn's eye from such a distance, the demon *looked* at him. Finn was sure of it. It did not move from where it had sunk to his knees, sucking Kestrall off, its cheeks hollowing and its mouth moving slowly, deliberately, up and down, up and down, but its brilliant green gaze was glued to the door—to the keyhole from which Finn was staring right back. As Kestrall's body gave another shudder, as his breathing grew louder and his cries closer together, the throbbing pain in Finn's hand cleared his mind enough that he was able to scramble to his feet.

He did not wait for the scene in the basement chamber to draw to a climax. He snatched up his love charm and ran, stumbling, gasping, almost sobbing, back to his own chamber, where he slammed the door and bolted it home.

Then he fell to his knees again and stroked once, twice, before collapsing onto the floor on his side, his body quivering helplessly in shock and his fingers wet with his cum.

CHAPTER FOUR

Finn groaned and stumbled out of his chamber the next morning, wondering if the previous night had been naught but a dream after all. He didn't even remember dragging himself to bed, so it stood to reason that he'd been there all along, caught in some feverish nightmare that thoughts of sex, of Jonti, had conjured up from the depths of his mind.

"Morning, Finn."

"M-Master Kestrall."

Kestrall didn't seem to notice Finn's hesitation. Indeed, he seemed inordinately cheerful, whistling as he went about the morning's chores.

Finn shook his head, blinking hard and then rubbing his eyes. Kestrall was actually *cleaning*.

"Master Kestrall? Are you . . . all right?"

"As well as ever," Kestrall smiled.

Finn's master was many things, but a morning person wasn't one of them—he often wasn't to be seen before noon, his habit usually being to stay up half or even all the night as he worked or studied. Finn scrutinized him from the corner of his eye as Kestrall continued scrubbing the kitchen table, now stunningly clear of books, paper, or strewed ingredients.

"You *never* clean," Finn accused him.

"Well . . ." At least Kestrall had the decency to blush. He ran his hands through his neatly bound hair. "I thought it was about time I started. I intend to begin instructing you properly, you know. I've taught you to read and to write, and you've watched as I've prepared charms and tinctures for customers. It's time I take over more of the cleaning and errands myself, to give *you* more time to do more work as befitting an apprentice."

"You didn't hire me as an apprentice." Finn watched, bemused, as his master continued to potter around the kitchen.

"Aye, but you've proven to have a good head on your shoulders. Besides, you've more than doubled my custom since I hired you. The customers like seeing a younger face around. It makes the place more approachable — especially as without you, the house would be unfit for anyone to see, let alone be invited in and sat down. And . . ."

"What?" Finn asked.

" . . . And I've been thinking you should know more about the magician's craft firsthand," said Kestrall slowly. "Better to know more about what you're working with. In this field, more than any other, ignorance can lead to peril."

"Peril? Like what?" Finn narrowed his eyes, watching carefully for his master's reaction.

"Oh . . . this and that." The back of Kestrall's neck turned a telltale red, and he pushed his eyeglasses up further on his nose — an unconscious, nervous gesture that Finn had seen hundreds of times before.

"Come to think of it, I did hear a thump last night — I thought I'd dreamed it," Finn tested.

"Never mind that," Kestrall replied a little too quickly. "Your studies will put you in no danger — I'll make sure of it. There's no need to fear injury."

It *hadn't* been a dream. Though his master was moving freely, no sign of having been hurt in any way, Finn was sure of it now — and his fingers itched to find the book he had given to Kestrall the day before.

That book had summoned the demon. He just knew it.

Finn had no time to search for the book that day, for both

he and his master were kept busy with a steady stream of customers. Together, they prepared charms and amulets for the people that came in to collect or order them.

A large boat had sailed into port the night before, and that meant sailors — they wanted talismans for good fortune on the water, protective amulets against fever and the sweating sickness, and love charms for their sweethearts waiting for them at home. It was also market day, and their home lay not a quarter hour's walk from the square. Kestrall's spells never failed to work, so it was said, and so young and old, men and women all visited his store, often encouraging passersby to notice the stream of visitors and grow curious enough themselves to see what made this particular magician so popular.

There were other magicians in the city, but they mostly lived on the other side of the river, and except to serve, common folk rarely ventured there, to the multi-storied townhouses and businesses that sold items far too expensive to contemplate throwing that much coin away on. Besides, no matter how busy he was, Kestrall rarely refused a customer. Finn had seen this happen only a scant handful of times — once to a woman who wanted a curse laid on a lover, and occasionally to men, usually young, who sought not love but coercion.

"Do your own cursing, if you must," Kestrall had told the woman, "but be wary — it may not only be your lover who is harmed." To the men, Kestrall simply folded his arms and shook his head, his tone cool. "That is not something that should be bought — if it can be done at all. Not here, nor anywhere, and pity the person who believes otherwise." It was the closest Finn had ever seen to anger from his master.

Now, however, Kestrall was as polite as ever, his good mood continuing throughout the day, even when sometime around lunch, Rosie came in for another charm for her ma, having gotten a friend to watch the market stall in her place for an hour or two. Thankfully, Finn was busy enough that he did not need an excuse to avoid her conversation, and anyway, there were other customers waiting alongside her. Kestrall always claimed the best amulets were those made as the need arose, so unless someone requested an item or incantation that was best done at night, or had to be created over several hours or days, customers often came in to wait while the magician, and today, his apprentice, worked alongside one another.

Though it was Finn's first time helping to prepare the charms himself, he was not nervous. He had stood by and watched for a long while now and knew what to do, only needing Kestrall's guidance to prepare those mixtures that were not so common.

"Only a couple of drops of the peppermint oil, it's strong," Kestrall warned later that day as Finn carefully measured out the right ingredients for an amulet to prevent miscarriage. "Then the teasel—plenty of that. Chamomile, too. Besides staving off bad humors, it has a pleasant smell and will cover the scent of the valerian."

"Yes, Master Kestrall."

"Good. I'll take this and perform the incantation downstairs. You go ahead and start mixing the necessary herbs for Mrs. Fletcher. Her husband's moved to a bigger shop and wants to protect against both thieves and fire. That will call for the—"

"Sage, I know. We're running low!" Finn called after him as Kestrall made his way downstairs.

The bell tinkled again over the shop door, and Finn, busy with measuring out the right quantity of sage, didn't look up. "Master Kestrall will be up shortly, as soon as he's finished with–"

"Actually, it was you who I wanted to see."

There was a loud clattering as Finn jerked, knocking the

mortar and pestle off the table with his elbow and onto the floor. "Jonti!"

"Sorry, didn't mean to distract you." Jonti looked as strong and handsome as always, the late afternoon sunlight coming through the windows turning his already blond hair to spun gold. His eyes seemed to dance as they gazed back at Finn. "Maybe you should rethink your apprenticeship, if you're making a habit of being so clumsy."

"Huh?" Finn could only gape unintelligently.

"The coins. In my shop yesterday. Remember?"

"Oh — yes. Of course. I remember."

"My master's closed up shop early today on account of him not feeling so good," Jonti continued, seemingly oblivious to Finn's discomfort. "He sent me here to ask Master Kestrall for something that'd help him sleep better. Says his bones are aching and keeping him up all night lately."

Finn nodded, only just managing to finally tear his gaze away from where he'd been counting the freckles dotting Jonti's nose. "For sleep. Right."

"I can wait, or come back later if you're busy. The pies at the market smell real nice — maybe I can bring you one. Master gave me money enough."

Finn shook his head. "Can't. Not when I'm working, the smell disrupts the magick of some of the ingredients we use."

"That's too bad." Jonti immediately brightened again. "Say, think I have enough here to pay you for that love charm as well? Might as well, while I'm here — 'specially if you're the one preparing it."

Finn froze. "What . . . do you mean?"

There appeared to be something just slightly coy about Jonti's smile as he shrugged. "Well, you need the practice, right? I heard you were helping now with the charms and all. Rosie told me when I passed by her stall a while ago. Congratulations, by the way."

"Er, thanks." Finn ducked his head. He was sure of it—Jonti was just waiting for Finn to make a move. But there was no way Finn would be able to confess his feelings for Jonti—not in a hundred years. Not without stuttering and tripping over his own feet and making a big fool of himself. That meant Jonti would have to go first. A good thing Finn hadn't burned that love charm last night after all. "Actually . . . you don't have to wait. I already made it. For you, I mean. Yesterday. Not that you have to—I mean, I'm still just the apprentice, so it might not be as good as . . ." He trailed off awkwardly, but Jonti rewarded him with a wide smile.

"Wow, that was fast. Thanks, Finn!"

"You're welcome," Finn muttered to the floor. Gods, why was it that Jonti was so damned radiant—and what was it he saw in Finn, of all people? "It's actually in my . . . I'll just go get it."

He brushed past Kestrall, back on his way into the kitchen with an armload of jars filled with various ingredients.

"Jonti, fancy seeing you here. Your master's not one to give anyone the day off work, is he?"

Finn listened to their voices as he searched for the amulet, wondering where he'd put it last night after returning to his bedchamber. There it was, on the small table beside the bed. He picked it up with trembling fingers, remembering to turn it upside down to check the fabric where he'd nearly burned it. There was a small smudge, but that was all. He stared down at the pouch in his hand, a half-formed idea growing in his mind. Did he dare?

" . . . Afraid we're fresh out of lemon balm," came Kestrall's voice, sounding apologetic. "But I'll send Finn down to get some more shortly. What say you come back in an hour? We'll have it ready for your master by then. Tell him to keep it somewhere near his bedside."

"Yes, sir."

42

Finn forced himself back into the kitchen, holding out his arm abruptly to Jonti. "Here you go."

"What's this, then?" Kestrall straightened his eyeglasses and peered down at the pouch, its red thread bold against the dull cream of the fabric. "Looks like a love—"

"It's nothing! I heard you needed more lemon balm?"

"Aye, we do, and more sage," Kestrall remembered. "There's some coin in my room—or maybe it was in here?" He glanced around absentmindedly.

"It's over there." Finn grabbed the purse from the middle shelf nearest the hallway, barely managing a choked goodbye to Jonti, and all but ran from the house.

Even so, he was determined now. He would find a way to summon that demon he'd seen last night in the basement, and he'd make it teach him everything he needed to know to please someone like Jonti.

Despite his determination, it was another several days before Finn worked up the courage to creep down to the basement while his master slept, and then only because he felt sure Kestrall would not wake. His master had stayed up all night previously, muttering to himself as he worked through probably yet more of the old spellbook, and he had not rested during that day either. He should sleep like the dead until morning, Finn reasoned.

Barefoot but still dressed in his day clothes, Finn crept downstairs. He bolted the basement door behind him and lit enough candles so that he could see the whole room well, sending shadows spiraling over the walls as the flames leaped and guttered, hissing slightly and dripping wax.

He did not have to search hard for the book. Although the basement contained the large worktable he had seen the very first time Kestrall had shown him the room, and a number of shelves crammed with books and loose sheets of parchment, the leather-bound tome somehow drew Finn to it, from where it lay half-buried under a sheaf of manuscripts, brittle and yellowed with age.

Taking a deep breath, Finn reminded himself that this quest would likely not be successful. He likely wouldn't be able to read the right part of the book at all—would probably not even manage to find the right section, if parts of the book were written in a foreign language. Finn's knowledge of runes and sigils was still rudimentary at best—and besides, even if the spell involved the reading of some incantation he *could* actually make out, it might also involve ingredients or rituals of which he as yet held no knowledge at all.

A loud sputtering from one of the candles behind him made Finn jump, and the book slid from his hands and onto the floor. Finn swore. If he'd damaged anything . . .

He bent over to pick the book up, and the page it had opened to immediately made his breath catch. Against all the odds, this was it—he knew this with all certainty.

The illustration was crude, but its meaning clear. There stood a horned being—a demon, of course—with inked lines showing its confinement to the magick circle where it had been summoned. It was naked, its arousal swollen and grotesque as the demon strained against its magickal bonds. In front of it stood another figure, this one a woman, her breasts bare. Unclothed to the waist, her arms were lifted toward the sky, her mouth open wide in invocation.

With fingers that now trembled, Finn turned the page, and saw with a jolt that the words were entirely readable. He stared, mouthing a few of them silently. None were words he recognized, but the alphabet was his own. If he managed to sound everything out properly . . . but no. Surely that could not be all. There must be preparations to make—herbs, potions, things done in the right order and at the right time of day or month. The illustration clearly depicted a summoning circle of some kind, which Finn had no idea how to correctly draw, and who knew what kind of other details the drawing did not show? It wouldn't even be guessing at the correct measurements of ingredients or layout of tools, for none were listed.

Disappointment stabbed at him. He didn't know what he'd been thinking. He, Finn, barely even an apprentice, summon a demon? Impossible, he snorted to himself, and made to close the book before he could carry this foolishness any further.

He couldn't. The stiff, cracked leather had somehow stuck fast, and now he couldn't push the cover down properly. Finn swore again, then looked around him. Well, he was here now, wasn't he? He'd already come this far, so he might as well draw a circle, say the incantation and see what happened. When nothing did, he could jam the book under the pile of manuscripts once more, maybe weigh it down with something heavier as well to try and close it properly, and never think of the incident again, knowing it would not lead him anywhere.

The floor had been recently swept, and it was no difficult task to draw a circle in the packed dirt with the other end of the broomstick leaning against one corner. At roughly equal points around the circle, Finn scrawled the only protective sigils he knew by heart, not knowing if they would be enough to contain a demon but figuring it wouldn't really matter, since one clearly wouldn't be appearing anyway. He was only doing this to put the thing from his mind once and for all.

Yes—it was purely to lay his curiosity to rest, he told himself firmly as he finished scratching out the last sigil. Then he stood, and as an afterthought looked through the glass jars of dried herbs stacked in an untidy row on a shelf. They were not labeled, but Finn picked one he thought he recognized, removed the lid, and took a tentative sniff, making sure his nose not too close.

Crushed fumitory. It was poisonous if ingested or burned in a confined space for too long, Kestrall had warned him once, which was why it was only kept downstairs, to be used by Kestrall himself as needed. It was also a protective herb — one that was supposed to keep evil at bay. Finn emptied a generous amount into a small wooden bowl and placed it by the door.

Deciding he was now as ready as he could make himself, Finn picked up the book again and walked nearer to the circle, making sure to stand a good arm's length away, feet not touching any of the lines. He took a deep breath.

"Fram eower miltsian, sealdnes mi . . ." He was already stumbling over the unfamiliar words but continued stubbornly. " . . . Forniman mod naole dreagon willa stepan awyrcan . . ." He coughed as one of the candles nearest him burned out, sending a spiral of smoke into the air. " . . . Fylstan frymdig baerlic artforan mi, gieldan mi, swicende meowle . . ." It was no short incantation, and Finn struggled for breath, hardly knowing where he was supposed to pause and where to allow the words to run together. His body felt suddenly heavy, his arms holding the book leaden. " . . . Onorettan men termen, meolce eower . . . mi weorlic," he finally finished, gasping a little and dizzy with lack of air.

He looked around cautiously. The circle remained empty, as did the rest of the small chamber. Nothing had happened.

With a sigh, Finn closed the book, which now seemed to snap shut in his hands with no difficulty at all. Really, what had he been expecting? Nothing at all, he told himself. He was no magician. Exasperated, he scuffed at the circle in the dirt before him with his foot. He would need to make sure to erase it and the sigils completely, leaving no trace of his little experiment.

He turned to fetch the broom, and from behind him, a voice

spoke into the quiet.

"Don't tell me *you're* the one who did this," it said.

CHAPTER FIVE

Finn screamed. A hand clapped itself over his mouth. "Silence, apprentice, or you'll wake your master."

With a burst of strength brought on by sheer panic, Finn wrenched free and dashed to the other end of the room, putting the worktable between himself and . . . it. The demon.

It was without doubt the same demon he had seen when he had been spying on Kestrall. It loomed over Finn, towering, more than twice the height and width of him, with flaming red hair and glittering green eyes that gazed at him coolly, not in the least perturbed in the face of Finn's terror.

"D-don't come any closer!" he said, his voice sounding weak even to his own ears.

The demon stepped casually out of the circle, barely deigning to look down at it. "I don't know if you thought *this* would contain me," it sniffed disdainfully, "but I'll have you know, I go wherever I please."

"Oh gods, oh gods, don't touch . . . I have fumitory!" Finn picked up the entire jar of herbs and brandished it before him like a weapon.

The demon cocked its head. "That is for banishing evil spirits. Also, it needs to be used correctly in spells for it to have any effect."

"Oh . . ." Finn stared at the jar. The demon had not moved again, and for all its condescension, it did not appear angry or even threatening. "I didn't know."

"There is much you clearly do not, apprentice . . . what name are you known by?"

"Finn," he replied numbly.

"Apprentice Finn." The demon seemed to taste the name as it spoke it, considering the sound of it on his lips.

"Are you . . . here to hurt me?"

"Whatever would I do that for?" The demon glanced idly around the room, eyeing the piles of books and unbound manuscripts, its gaze then moving across the collection of dried herbs and various candles.

"Well . . . you're a demon, aren't you?"

"Excuse *you*. I'm an incubus, mind your tongue," it snapped, its attention back on Finn.

Finn gave a short, shocked laugh. "What's the difference?"

"I'm not here to torture you, for one. Though as I *am* capable of certain magickal feats, I'd suggest not insulting me like that again," said the incubus, still a little peevishly. "Now, why don't we start over?" He smiled with exaggerated politeness. "Greetings and salutations. I'm an *incubus*, and lest we forget, *you're* the one who summoned me here, oh noble apprentice. I assume you'd invite me to sit, but as you can see, you have a distinct lack of chairs." He waved a hand around the chamber.

Finn was still shaken but now not quite so afraid. Sarcasm was at least something he understood. "I didn't mean to summon you . . . well, all right, I did, but I didn't truly believe—"

"Yes, well, be careful what you wish for and all that." The incubus' tone had changed, becoming more languid and curious as he looked Finn over. "Quite the ambitious one, aren't you? It takes more than idle curiosity to summon anything at all, you know, even for the more skilled of magicians. Although, if I may say so, that silly little invocation you no doubt spoke—yes, don't think I don't see that book lying over there—was not as responsible for my appearance as you may believe."

"So, what, you just . . . decided to pop in for a visit then?"

Finn's voice was still shaky, but he managed to inject a little sarcasm of his own, about which the incubus seemed oddly pleased.

"Something like that." He gazed at Finn steadily. "I was summoned here by you, that much is true. Think of it as knocking on my door, if you like. Now, are you going to tell me why you did so?"

"I saw you with my master the other night," Finn admitted.

"I know. I saw you too," said the incubus with a sudden grin that was all teeth. "Enjoyed the show, did you? Don't answer that—the fact I'm standing here again now is answer enough. And I promise you this, you missed out on a great deal more than what little *you* saw of it. Oh yes—even for an incubus, I'd like to think I'm *very* good at what I do."

"So . . . you're *not* going to hurt me then?"

"Whatever would I do that for?" The incubus seemed genuinely perplexed. "Pain brings me no sustenance, so what good is it to the likes of me?"

"You hurt my master," Finn countered, suspicion still making him wary.

The incubus raised an eyebrow. "Only because he wanted it, I assure you. Pain can bring pleasure, under certain circumstances." He grinned again, rolling his shoulders. "So can fear. A little rush, a taste of danger to heighten the senses can do *marvelous* things for the body. Some people seek it out, and under such conditions, I'm only too happy to oblige." He waved a hand almost nonchalantly. "But pain for pain's sake, for cruelty, is not my domain, nor will it do anything to nourish me. As I said, I am no demon. No," he continued, "I am in the business of pleasure. *That* is what nourishes me." The look he gave Finn then was downright predatory.

Finn gulped, his mouth suddenly gone dry. "And you bring pleasure . . . to anyone?"

"Well . . . anyone I happen to like enough who wants it.

Anyone who asks — nicely. Are *you* asking nicely, Finn?" The incubus walked closer. Finn took a step back, and another as the incubus continued his approach, until Finn's back was flush against the shelving at the end of the room. "Let me guess. You wanted a taste of what you saw for yourself. A young man, on the cusp of a world as yet unknown . . . you're in love, or as close to love as you know it at such an age. I can see it so clearly in your face."

"How . . . how can you — "

"The world of men is no mystery to me," the incubus purred. "I've seen many things, and heard many things, and *done* many things. Do you, too, want to be done, Finn?"

"You . . . you're a little . . ." Finn could not quite summon the courage to tell the incubus he wasn't really Finn's type. Closer to his master in years, for one, and physically far more intimidating than Finn was comfortable with, for another. Even as he recognized a spark of desire in him, the thought of pain, of domination, brought him nothing but apprehension.

"Hmm . . . turn away for a moment, will you, Finn?"

He didn't know why he obeyed, but he did. Finn's back was turned to the demon for only the space of a few breaths before he felt a light tap on his shoulder.

"Perhaps something like this is more to your taste."

Just like that, the incubus had changed his shape. When Finn turned back around, a far younger man greeted his gaze, roughly the same age and height as Finn himself. The incubus' hair was now as black as night. His face was narrow and sharp, his build slight. Only his dramatically pale skin and long, slanted eyes were the same — these still a wicked, gleaming green that looked Finn up and down with not a shred of modesty.

Finn shivered as the incubus raised a finger, stroking it softly down his cheek. It was a touch that seared him, seemingly from beneath his skin. Despite himself, his body strained against that touch, instinctively hungering for more. "I . . . I shouldn't't've—"

"Probably not, but now that I'm here, it would go against my nature—and yours as well, it would appear—to just leave without having a bit of fun. Don't you think, my dear apprentice?"

Finn was silent.

"I'll need more than that." The incubus' eyes narrowed. "Summoned or not, I take only what is freely given, or it means naught to me. Do you understand?"

"Yes . . ." Finn wasn't sure he did, but the word crept from his mouth before he could think.

"Then say it."

"Yes."

"Yes, what?"

"I want . . ."

"Yes?"

" . . . Want you. To teach me things. To show me . . ." He couldn't bring himself to finish, but the incubus seemed more than satisfied.

"Good." His hand was suddenly around Finn's throat, squeezing just tight enough to prevent further speech. "Because I want something from you, too. So glad we have an accord." His mouth came down to press hard against Finn's, insistent, desiring.

Finn parted his lips to gasp, and the incubus' tongue slipped inside his mouth, sliding up against Finn's, making his heart pound. He forgot how to breathe. He forgot how to think.

"Your first lesson," the incubus spoke as he finally pulled away, allowing Finn a little space. "How it feels to have another's touch on you, not only in base lust, but from true desire. Shall I continue?"

Dazed, Finn managed a nod, and the incubus guided him

to the center of the room. A hand undid the laces at the top of his shirt.

"Skin to skin," the incubus said, and pulled the shirt over Finn's head in one fluid motion, quickly following suit with his own. He kissed Finn again, their chests brushing, sending little jolts through Finn's body.

Clumsily, shyly, Finn began to kiss the incubus in return, wondering if he was doing it right, then soon deciding he no longer cared. Something about the incubus was making his limbs feel slow and warm, almost like he was asleep, even though he was certain this could be no dream.

The incubus pressed against him even closer, almost toppling Finn over before supporting him with one arm at Finn's back. The other was busy roving Finn's upper body, ghosting over his ribs, exploring the dips and hollows of his neck down to his collarbone.

Finn made a choked noise of protest when the incubus broke away again, then gasped aloud when the incubus flashed a grin and began kissing elsewhere on Finn's body. His tongue found Finn's nipples. Finn jerked. The incubus held him still, keeping him close, and grazed the area with his teeth, biting down gently. Even so, it was enough to make Finn let out a strangled moan.

"Is this . . . is it . . ."

"What people do to one another, for one another? Oh yes. And more. *So* much more." The incubus was pushing gently, guiding Finn so that he stood with the wall at his back again. He inhaled deeply, regarding Finn's disheveled form with obvious approval. "Ahh, this is delightful. So long since I've had a blushing virgin in my arms," he sighed. "The smell alone . . ." He closed his eyes, tipping his head back, then looked back at Finn. "Your desire is the sweetest elixir to me. A golden nectar like no other on this earth."

Finn wasn't sure he understood, but could only moan

again as the incubus continued its appraisal of Finn's body with teeth and tongue, here licking, there nipping lightly until Finn was panting, his trousers almost unbearably tight where his arousal strained against its confines.

Thus far, the incubus had left this part of Finn untouched. Now he stroked his hand softly over the fabric. Finn whimpered.

"The impatience of youth." The incubus smirked. "So anxious to have it all, and as quickly as possible, even when patience is sometimes its own reward." His hand moved, torturously slowly.

Finn gripped the incubus' shoulders, not sure whether he was trying to make him stop or press down harder, and at the same time needing something to hold on to simply to keep himself still. He felt his heart would leap from his chest if he did not.

"Now you see what drives men to such impulses," the incubus continued, his voice low and soft. "Is it what you imagined? Does it make your blood sing in your veins?"

"I thought . . . I thought . . ." Finn could barely make his mouth move to form the sounds.

"You thought it would bring pain. You thought all men crave power over others and derive pleasure from forcing another to submit. From their shame. You were wrong." The incubus stroked harder, his motions now more purposeful.

"You . . . with my master—" Finn gasped, struggling to find the words.

"Rest assured, I gave your master only what he desired, just as I am giving you your desire. I see the inner truths of men, and when I choose, I *fulfill* them."

"Please, oh gods please, I'm going to . . ."

"I know, my dear. Try to hold on just a *little* longer, for my hunger is not satisfied just yet." The incubus gave a little squeeze, chuckling against Finn's neck as he jumped, then moved his fingers to undo the lacing at the top of Finn's trousers. "Though I do appreciate the enthusiasm," he added. He pushed the material down, stripping Finn to his thighs. "Don't be afraid to reciprocate. Desire is not limited to only one."

The words sank in, and Finn fought the heaviness of limbs to return the gesture. Together, they divested one another of what little remained on their bodies until both stood entirely bared to one another. Finn's cock was already leaking, quivering against the incubus' touch like a live thing.

"*Please . . .*" Finn was desperate now, the tide rising in him and threatening to crash outward. If what he'd felt several nights ago had been intense, this was near impossible to withstand. The incubus' hands were everywhere now, yanking him close, grabbing his hair, their bodies straining against one another, cheek to cheek, chest to chest, hip to hip, grinding down and making Finn cry out.

"Good, *good*, just like that, you're so close, my dear, I can all but *taste* it–"

Finn shuddered, his legs suddenly giving way, and the incubus held him and smothered the next cry with his mouth as Finn's release overtook him — as they both came, still holding one another tightly, their seed spurting and then mingling together, coating their stomachs and sliding slowly back down over flesh that was slick with sweat.

"I'm . . . you're . . ." Finn could still barely speak.

The incubus held him as he continued to tremble. "Breathe. You'll pass out if you don't. Magick affects the body in different ways."

"Magick," said Finn blearily.

"You summoned me, and then I fed on your desire. Now your spirit is drained and your energy depleted. You need to rest so that it can restore itself."

"Oh." Finn closed his eyes and leaned his head on the

incubus' shoulder.

"*Finn*." The incubus was insistent. "I cannot stay."

"Huh?"

"I cannot exist for long like this, in your realm, and you cannot exist with me. It goes against Natural Law."

"I don't understand," Finn mumbled. He felt dizzy again, like he had when he'd first read the spell to summon the incubus, the room spinning even behind closed eyelids.

"I know. Here." The incubus' manner was oddly gentle as he guided Finn safely to the ground before his body could give out entirely. "Listen to me closely, Finn." His tone was serious now. "Do not summon me again. Using hedge-witchery, amulets and other trinkets, is one thing. But deep magick — the kind that causes different beings to exist in the same space for a time — is not something to be trifled with. I do not harm humankind, but I cannot help but take. Such is my nature."

Finn struggled to understand. His thoughts, his words, were slow in coming. "I . . . I can't call you again?"

"No." The incubus' voice was firm.

Finn opened his eyes, upset without quite knowing why. "I won't ever see you again?"

"Well . . . I didn't say that."

Warmth crept slowly into Finn's chest. "When?" he asked simply.

"When I deem the time to be right. Here." He passed Finn his clothes. "Clean yourself up, put these back on. Your master would not be pleased to find you here."

"Shit . . ." Finn fumbled awkwardly with the fabric, the incubus dressing himself and then helping Finn until they were both more or less clothed again, though it was quite beyond Finn's ability to re-lace his own trousers or his shirt. No matter — he knew he would sleep as soon as he lay down, assuming he even made it to his bed.

"Finn."

"What?" He was finding it difficult to concentrate.

"Natural Law. No matter what I may wish, no matter how much you may desire, I can appear before you like this only thrice. That is not something in my power to alter. I will not waste those chances. Neither should you. Do you understand?" He stared at Finn, unblinking.

Slowly, Finn nodded.

"Good enough. Do not call me . . . but if you call *for* me, I might just consent to answer," the incubus said, the playfulness back in his voice, and took a deliberate step back.

"Wait!"

The incubus paused, his expression curious now. "What?"

"Your name. Tell me your name."

"My—" The incubus appeared taken aback. "Why would you want to know something like that?"

"Because, I . . . I just do. Please," Finn begged, and the incubus seemed to consider the request for a long moment. It dragged out between them until Finn was afraid the incubus would not speak again at all.

"My true name is not something any human should know, and even if you did, it would be beyond your ability to speak it," he said finally.

Finn tasted bitter disappointment, though once again, he could not find the reason. "Please," he whispered again.

The incubus blinked. "I am an incubus," he said, and the surprise on his face was mirrored in his voice, as though he himself had not expected to give an answer at all. "I exist in the night, and my power grows strong under starlight. I come when invited and feed on hunger, desire, flesh that trembles for the touch of another. For that reason . . . you may call me Tarric."

At this final word, Finn's vision dimmed. Though his eyes remained open, the chamber grew hazy and his body

suddenly much colder. He panicked and let out a yell of terror, his limbs jerking as he struggled to draw breath.

By the time Finn's sight returned a moment later, the incubus had vanished. So had the book that had been used to summon him, he saw, as well as the magick circle from which the
incubus had appeared. All seemed just as it had been when
Finn had first entered the chamber, however long ago that
was. It might have only been minutes, it might have been the
entire night. Down in the basement, there was no way of telling. Only one candle was still lit, flickering sluggishly.

Slowly, painfully, Finn picked the candle up and made
himself walk to the door, heaving it shut behind him. The trip
back to the top of the stairs seemed far too long, and Finn shivered uncontrollably as he stumbled up. Then, through sheer
effort of will, he groped his way on through the darkness, the
single flame barely enough to light his way, back to his bedchamber.

There, he blew out the candle and collapsed onto the bed,
and for a long time, he knew no more.

CHAPTER SIX

"Finn. *Finn.* Can you hear me?"

Finn groaned. His throat was raw and his body throbbed. He hadn't even opened his eyes, but he could already tell it was far too bright. "Go 'way," he mumbled.

"Here. Drink."

A cup was pushed against his lips. "Huh?" Water, mixed with something bitter and powdery. Finn scowled and tried to push the cup away, but the hand holding it was insistent.

"Come, now. All of it," the voice coaxed.

Master Kestrall. Blearily, Finn cracked his eyes open. "What happened? What time is it?"

"You had a fever. You didn't wake all yesterday. It's morning again."

"What do you mean?" Finn sat up, Kestrall easing him onto an extra pillow he placed beneath his neck. Memories were returning, slowly. Like scattered pieces of a dream, they revealed themselves in broken flashes first. A book. An invocation. Sputtering candles. An incubus . . ."Tarric."

"Who's Tarric?"

Finn looked around at the daylight streaming in from the doorway leading to the hall. Dust motes floated on the air. He looked back at his master. Rounded eyeglasses slightly askew, soft lines around his eyes and on his forehead. Everything was normal. And yet, nothing would ever be normal—not ever again.

"Nobody. A dream. I've already forgotten it." Even if Finn forgot everything else in his life, last night would be etched into his mind for as long as he drew breath.

"Finish this."

Finn's hands were not entirely steady, but he managed to hold the cup without spilling the mixture. He drank the rest down, making a face but knowing it was for the best.

"Good. How are you feeling?" Kestrall placed a large hand on Finn's forehead.

"Achy. Tired. I slept for that long?" he asked, aware now of what his master had said earlier.

"Aye, and very worried I was for you, too. The physicker has already come and gone. He said it was a spring fever, something the younger ones often die from." Kestrall set the cup down by the bedside. "I closed the shop. Told everyone to come back later."

"Your customers—"

"Will do as they're told," Kestrall finished. "Many of them know of you, Finn. They like you. They told me to look after you as long as it took and not to worry about anything else."

Finn looked down at his hands. "I'm sorry, Master Kestrall," he said softly.

"Don't be daft, lad. I'm just glad you're all right. I . . . you know you're more to me than just an apprentice." The magician sounded uncharacteristically hesitant.

"Master Kestrall?"

"Do you remember the day I took you in off the street?"

Finn nodded. They rarely spoke of this between them— Kestrall himself was a friendly but private man, Finn knew, and one who believed a man's past was his own. He understood Finn's own need for privacy in turn, and so their conversations were most often limited to the present.

"You were . . . well, dirty. Small. Underfed," Kestrall continued. "But even then, I saw you had potential. I could see you were clever and determined, and better still, that you had a good heart." Finn made to protest at this, but his master held up a hand, forestalling his answer. "Nay, be quiet a moment and just listen. I took you in as an errand boy that day, though you proved yourself capable of more than that. But it's not just that you're my apprentice. I know I've never told you this, but I think of you as family. Maybe you've never had a family, maybe you don't really know what that word means yet, deep down. Still, this is something I should have told you long since. If anything were to happen to you, especially for something I did—"

"What?" Finn knew his mouth was agape.

Kestrall looked at Finn, his brown eyes troubled. "I promised you would be safe," he said quietly. "I swore to you nothing would harm you in my work—"

"Nothing has," Finn interrupted again, still confused and growing slightly panicked now, wondering if Kestrall had found him out.

"Even so. If something did," his master insisted. "If you were threatened, if you ever felt unsafe, if . . ." He trailed off, pushing at his eyeglasses agitatedly.

"Master Kestrall . . . I'm fine. Look at me. I'm safe. Nothing has harmed me. Nothing is going to harm me. It was just a fever." Finn gestured down at himself. "This wasn't your fault. Just a spring fever, like the physicker said. There's nothing . . . I don't fear you, or your work, or this house. Nothing at all." Finn tried to assure him.

"Are you sure?" Kestrall took a breath. "You know you could tell me if you felt endangered or even so much as uneasy . . . I would never put you at risk for the sake of my work. Do you understand that?" Now it was Kestrall's turn to look away. "I know I can be . . . driven, sometimes, perhaps to the point of obliviousness. There are days where I get so lost in my work that I become unaware of what goes on around me. You've known that for a long time. I may have made all the amulets and tinctures and charms over the years, but *you're* really the one who's been running this place. Making sure I have all the tools I need, welcoming customers, ensuring I eat once in a while." Kestrall snorted in self-reproach. "I would make an even worse master magician if I couldn't even guarantee my own apprentice's safety in return."

"Master Kestrall!" Finn sat upright, unaided by the pillows now. "I'm *fine*. And I will be fine. You've taken care of me so far. You let me stay. You taught me things I needed to know, taught me to read . . . you gave me a *home*." Finally, Finn allowed himself to say it. No matter what Kestrall said, Finn had known it for years—ever since that first day, in fact, clean and standing upright in the clothes his master had given him. A gift more valuable than any amount of coin. "A real home, the first time I've had in my life that I can remember. You haven't put me in danger. I promise."

Kestrall stared.

Finn stared back. "I *promise*," he said again.

Kestrall stood. "Right." He pushed his hair back from his face. "Right," he said again, and now he sounded more cheerful, like his old absentminded self. "I'll just get you some more water. The fever's passed, but you need to keep drinking. Physicker's orders—and mine, too."

He gave no chance for objection, for all that Finn felt plenty strong enough now to get out of bed. His energy was returning by the minute and his head felt perfectly clear again. Whistling, Kestrall left the room, and Finn looked around, this time more deliberately.

Still the same shelf above his bed with the well-used magickal primers. Still the same bedside table with drawers full of candles, parchment, writing tools, everything a young magician's apprentice should have close at hand. Still the same wardrobe with the same well-mended but respectable clothes. Absolutely nothing had changed—and at the same time, everything had.

A tiny glint of color caught Finn's eye then, and he scrambled out of bed to walk over and examine it. An old hook in the wall just outside his door. It had always hung empty, unused by either Finn or his master.

Not this morning.

The pouch was undyed hemp, but the silver threading gleamed in the sunlight—a color rarely used in amulets, and usually only for those that called for strong protection against ill intent or malevolent workings. Finn sniffed.

White sage, certainly. Rue. And something else, something deeper and more bitter. Finn inhaled deeply, thinking hard. Only then did it come to him.

Crushed fumitory.

The days and weeks passed, spring melding into summer. Finn continued his work with Kestrall, and seeing that Finn was already competent in creating most of the commonplace herbal charms, his master moved them on to amulets made from other materials such as clay or stone and inscribed with various runes. It was like learning another language all over again, and Finn went to bed at the end of each day with his head reeling and sigils dancing before his eyes.

As the hot summer continued, city preparations for the harvest festival began, though it would not be held for several weeks yet. Kestrall had decided that this year, for the first time, he would set up temporary shop in Market Square alongside his fellow craftsmen and artisans—selling his wares side by side with potters and painters, jewelers and engravers, apothecarists and fortune-tellers, weavers and carvers. There too would be many people crowding into the city from the countryside, along with those who commonly traveled from town to town, from farmers and peddlers to jesters and minstrels. There would be stories, songs, dancing, and of course, feasting, and the city was bustling with talk and preparations.

For Kestrall and Finn, this meant long hours creating enough supplies in between serving their regular customers to last the full festival day, since there would not be time or space enough to create their wares behind their allocated stall. Finn had barely enough time to think, let alone make an attempt to call for an incubus named Tarric, however much the idea nagged at him. Besides, had the incubus not told Finn that he must not summon him? Tarric had made it clear that, *if* he ever showed up in Finn's life again, it would be solely on his own terms, not Finn's.

And so the season drew to its zenith, and life went on much as it always had since Finn had come to work for Master Kestrall. Although Finn saw Jonti in passing plenty of times, these were only in brief snatches, and Jonti had not mentioned anything more about the love charm Finn had made for him, or anything much to do with Finn at all. This made Finn wonder if, despite Jonti now having the love charm, he had actually intended Finn to use it for himself. Was Jonti perhaps waiting for Finn to make the first move, and keeping his distance from Finn now because Finn hadn't said or done anything to encourage him? If so, Jonti was being patient indeed . . .

The thought occurred one night with such abruptness that Finn groaned, appalled at his own stupidity. Of *course*. All along, Finn had been waiting for Jonti, when really it was Jonti who wanted Finn to act first. The love charm had been a hint, and one that had gone right over Finn's head, just like the inexperienced idiot he was.

Still, Finn hesitated. He understood now that bed sport was not something that had to be painful or humiliating — that two people could both experience pleasure from it. The incubus — Finn shivered at the thought — had seen thoroughly to that. He was no longer afraid of another's touch, and even thought he might work up the courage with Jonti to . . . well, to give back in return, though the notion of how exactly to go about this still escaped him.

Still, that did not mean Finn was ready to fall into bed with someone as self-assured and handsome—beautiful, really—as Jonti. How could Finn—short, skinny, woefully inexperienced Finn—compare to the likes of Jonti, who was popular with everyone and no doubt had plentiful firsthand knowledge to draw on? Would Finn not stutter and fumble as he usually did around him, and completely fail to please him? Finn barely knew his way around his own body, much less someone else's. Should Jonti not laugh at him and brush him off after realizing that Finn had no idea what he was doing in bed? Finn snorted at himself in derision. More to the point, he'd have about as much chance of guiding someone around and inside of him as he would if he'd been completely blind.

That night, too hot to sleep anyway, Finn tossed and turned, hating himself and despairing of the idea that he would ever manage to tell Jonti how he felt, knowing how underprepared he would be for whatever followed.

Worse yet, despite himself, he was half-hard at the mere thought of being in bed with Jonti. His scalp tingled. Sweat formed around the base of his skull.

Finn sighed and kicked the blanket all the way off. Well, maybe he should just bring himself to release, though his heart was not in it—at least then he might be able to sleep, though it would hardly help to cool him down.

Half-heartedly, he began touching himself, lightly at first, trying to take his mind off his own failings and think only of Jonti. Blond hair. Dancing blue eyes. Sun-golden skin and those smattering of freckles across a surprisingly sweet, up-turned nose.

A narrow face with razor-sharp cheekbones and a wide, teasing smile.

Finn groaned. It was not Jonti in his mind's eye now, but

the incubus. He tried to pull back from the image, to replace it with thoughts of Jonti, but couldn't. His breath quickened. He imagined the incubus' silkily trailing hair, his soft voice, almost a hiss over his skin. He felt that sharp green gaze boldly roaming his flesh.

Finn shivered, not with cold but in the beginnings of real pleasure. Gods, but Tarric had been something else, something Finn would never have even dared to imagine. Now he couldn't get the incubus out of his head. Truth be told, he hadn't been able to ever since that night, and not merely because of the physical pleasure he had experienced. Was it magick that made the incubus so compelling, the image of him burned into Finn's mind?

Did it matter? Finn stroked harder and one hand stole up to pinch his nipple between forefinger and thumb, sending a jolt all the way down his body. His cock gave an answering jerk, making Finn twist to muffle a cry into his pillow.

The tension in his body built, and finally Finn gave up, the incubus' name on his lips, little more than a whimper in the dark. *"Tarric."*

"You called?"

Finn shrieked.

Just as it had once before, a hand came over his mouth. "Hush, apprentice."

"I—I can't see you!" Finn cried, panicking. It was pitch black—he had not lit any candles, and the disembodied voice seemed to move from here to there, making it impossible for Finn to place where exactly it came from.

"And you won't need to," came the smooth reply. "I know where you are just fine. *All* of you," the incubus added suggestively.

"Wait, Tarric, I can't, you said not to—"

"Shh. Calm yourself and all will be well. I came here of my own volition. Your spirit will not be depleted as it was previously. You are safe with me . . . well, as safe as you'd like to be." Finn could not see Tarric licking his lips suggestively, but he was almost sure that was what the incubus was doing.

"Are you . . . is this—"

"Enough questions." Tarric's voice came suddenly next to Finn's ear, making him jump. The incubus must be crouched right next to him now. Finn felt the tickle of his breath on him, and goosebumps rose on his flesh. "Listen closely now, for this is your second lesson." Tarric's voice dropped lower until it was almost a whisper. *"Spirits of desire, gather near. In this spell I invoke thee, in light and in shadow, by sun and by starlight . . ."*

It was part of the invocation to a love charm, Finn realized at once — the one he himself had performed when he'd made his own — and Tarric forestalled his next question. "Of course, in the art of lovemaking, of giving and receiving pleasure, it helps to know your lover's body even in the blackest of nights." A slender hand moved to cup Finn's arousal and softly stroke, taking over from where Finn had left off. "Don't be afraid of the dark. Embrace it."

Finn shivered again as the incubus moved atop him. He was already unclothed, and it took the space of a moment for Finn to all but tear off his own bedclothes. Tarric made a noise of approval. "Good. Fortune favors the bold."

Finn huffed a laugh. "I don't think that saying means—"

"Hush. Or on second thought, don't. Your cries are music to my ears. I would dearly like to hear them again this night."

Finn felt himself grow red, but the incubus gave him no time to dwell on his embarrassment. Tarric rocked against him, gently at first but then with more fervor as their cocks ground together between their bodies. Finn tipped back his head to moan, and Tarric seemed to drink it in, sighing in pleasure.

He guided Finn's hands over his body, encouraging him to touch Tarric in return. His cock was already hot and a little slippery in Finn's hands, and Finn let out a breath, rubbing the pre-cum over his fingers, half in amazement. *I did this?*

"Yes, my dear. Oh, yes. Don't stop now."

Emboldened, Finn ran his hands over the rest of Tarric's body—something he had not quite dared to do when last they had met. Now he dragged his fingers through the incubus' hair, even bringing it to his nose to smell it, sweet and faintly spicy. He ran his fingertips down Tarric's spine, feeling the bumps of each individual bone beneath the skin. He mapped out Tarric's ribcage and then moved down again, squeezing Tarric's thighs and wrapping his legs around the incubus' hips to lock their bodies together, increasing the friction. Tarric hissed and Finn felt the spasming of his cock between them, more fluid leaking out and smearing, warm and slick, over their lower bodies.

"Finn . . . I'm going to touch you now, inside of you. Is that what you want?"

Finn gasped and nodded, the thought alone making him shudder in renewed pleasure. "Will you . . . will it . . ."

It wasn't fear of pain that made him hesitate, but simply that he was close now, so close, and he didn't want that feeling to go away, or to lessen even one bit. " . . . Hurt?"

"A little. I will guide you through it."

Finn nodded again, then yelped as he felt a finger stroke his crease. It was wet with something slick and oily, and slightly cold. It pressed inside him slowly—not painful yet or even rough, just unfamiliar. Finn held himself still.

"Relax," came Tarric's voice, dark with pleasure. "Don't try to hold yourself still for me if you don't want to. I will not harm you."

"Oh . . ." Another finger, just as slick, was added to the first. They pushed in a little deeper now, and Finn squirmed. He trusted Tarric, but if this was what all the fuss was about, he wasn't sure making love by allowing someone else inside of him was something he really —

Finn gasped. The fingers had brushed against something, something entirely new. Whatever it was, it made Finn jump again, and not just in surprise. From his throat came a reflexive groan, more guttural than any of his last.

The incubus chuckled. "Like that, did you?"

"Yes — oh yes — can you — " Finn babbled as Tarric's fingers pressed harder, a little deeper yet again. Finn's eyes were open wide and staring even though there was nothing to see. His fists opened and closed, nails digging hard into his palms, cock painfully hard as pre-cum continued to spill from the tip and drip steadily down onto his thighs and belly.

He was about to come, about to say so, when the fingers abruptly withdrew. The sudden emptiness was an unwelcome sensation, raw, and Finn could have almost wept. "Don't — no — please — "

"Patience, young apprentice," replied the incubus, shifting his position atop Finn's body, and he sounded slightly breathless himself, a trembling note to his voice. "The best is yet to come. Are you ready?"

As though Finn could have given any reply but a desperate, needy affirmative. He knew, vaguely, what was coming, and if Tarric had promised him it would not hurt much, if it would really be better even than what had come before it . . .

Slowly, the incubus lowered himself and pushed in, his cock pressing past the contracting muscles of Finn's entrance. Finn's spine immediately stiffened.

"Deep breath, my dear. It will pass, shh, don't try to fight it, else the pain will only grow worse . . ." Tarric stroked Finn's face, reassurance in his touch. "Keep your body relaxed. Don't push, don't strain. Breathe with it . . ."

Finn tried to do as instructed, taking a steadying breath and making sure his back remained flat on the bed. The pain ebbed a little.

"Yes . . . that's the way of it . . ." Tarric hadn't moved again, and Finn grasped the incubus' arms.

"You can . . . if you want . . ." Curse it, he didn't really know what he wanted, what he was asking for, but Tarric seemed to understand.

"Close your eyes. You do not need your sight to feel me, here in the darkness," he whispered.

Finn obeyed, and gently, the incubus shifted his hips, a slight back and forth motion that started in another brief spurt of pain, and ended in —

"Aah!" The sound tore its way from Finn's mouth. "Oh. *Ooh* . . ."

"It is to your liking then, I take it?"

"Gods, oh gods —"

"And have no doubt, your pleasure more than doubles mine. *Delicious*, simply divine . . . give me more. *More.*" Tarric's last word ended on a growl. He moved faster, panting slightly, and Finn could picture the incubus in his mind — Tarric's mouth open in pleasure and triumph, his eyes glittering. Finn even saw himself reflected in them, two tiny versions trapped, gloriously, beneath the incubus' body, writhing and shuddering, as the sensation deep in his stomach built up and up, reaching fever pitch.

It was this final image that was his undoing. With another jolt, he came, spilling against Tarric's belly. The incubus' hands grasped at Finn's shoulders only a moment later, clenching the skin with near-bruising force as he climaxed, leaving Finn to tremble at the warm, sticky burst flooding inside of him.

CHAPTER SEVEN

"You may light a candle now, if you wish." The voice sounded lazy and sated.

Finn's body, once he'd lain still a while and remembered how to breathe normally, was heavy but not particularly sore, though his back was stiff and something inside him felt stretched and tender. He was sleepy, but not past the point of being unable to think or move. He fumbled for the tinderbox.

The wavering flame revealed Tarric, sitting cross-legged at the foot of the bed, looking like a cat who'd just gotten the . . .

Cream. Finn flushed.

"Don't tell me you've had a sudden concern for your modesty *now*. A bit late for that, don't you think?"

"No . . ." Finn pulled his nightshirt back over his head anyway, though in part because he was beginning to grow cooler now that the sweat was drying on his skin.

Tarric stretched, again looking oddly cat-like, and Finn considered. "Can I ask you a question?"

"Whatever you like," Tarric yawned, indolent and seemingly completely unconcerned with his own nudity.

"Last time we . . . met, I could barely move after. I caught a fever, and Master Kestrall said I slept for more than a day. Why isn't the same thing happening to me now?"

"Last time, you summoned me. I chose to answer that summons, but it was your energy that was responsible for it. This time, I came using my own methods."

"I see." He didn't really, at least not in full, but what was magick to Finn was clearly far more ordinary to the likes of

Tarric. "But my master summoned you too . . . didn't he?" Finn remembered then. "Nothing happened to him after."

"Your master is a great deal older than you, and a great deal more knowledgeable. The less you understand what you're doing in a summoning, the more your body will pay for it."

Finn was quiet for a while as he thought about this, wondering if he would at some point truly become a magician himself in the future as Kestrall thought, and what that might mean for him. In a score of years, would Finn really be in Kestrall's shoes, or somewhere close to it?

That reminded him of another thought. "I read about you, you know," he said to Tarric. "Or tried, anyway. About incubuses."

"Oh? Do tell—I just *love* being educated about myself, especially by humans." Tarric grinned, taking the sting out of his words. "It's incu*bi*, incidentally. But I mean it. By all means, continue."

"Well . . ." Finn thought back to the books he'd managed to track down. He hadn't been able to bring himself to ask for such books at the Crow's Nest, for fear word would get back to Kestrall or that the master bookkeeper—or worse still, Jonti—would ask awkward questions. If there were any books in the house on the subject, they were not kept upstairs, and he certainly wasn't about to ask Kestrall about it—not after that protective charm left dangling beside Finn's bedchamber door. Kestrall might not have known that Finn had summoned Tarric, but he was clearly aware his apprentice had tried to do *something* he wasn't supposed to, and if Finn mentioned too much, would almost certainly put two and two together. Besides, even had Finn been entirely blameless, he was not about to initiate a conversation with Kestrall—not only his master, but the closest thing to a father he had—about bedsport. So, in the end, Finn had gone to one of the smaller bookshops Kestrall only rarely frequented, spending several precious silver pieces on just two books — all there was to be found — about ghosts, spirits, and other non-human entities. He had found no books at all only on incubuses, and what passages he had found sounded faintly ridiculous, even to Finn's admittedly patchy knowledge.

" . . . Not a lot, to be honest," Finn finished. "The information I did find didn't exactly . . . er, match up."

Tarric waved a hand. "I'm all ears."

Finn rushed ahead. "Both the books I found said you — incubuses I mean — were evil spirits. They said they crushed people . . . well, women . . . in their sleep, so that they couldn't move or even speak. The women all went mad after or died right then, sometimes from suffocation and sometimes from their heart giving out. And the incubus attacked them by . . . um . . . well, stealing their life force and, uh . . . drying them out."

Tarric arched an inquisitive eyebrow. "By *drying out*, I assume those deeply learned scholars are referring to incubi forcing themselves upon the poor, helpless women until they were literally ravished to death."

"I guess."

"And has that been your experience?"

"Well, no. For one thing, I'm not a woman."

"Really? Do tell."

Finn ignored the sarcasm. "All the books said the victims were women," he pressed. "So . . . um, do you . . . "

"I lie with whom I please," said Tarric smoothly. "And it pleases me to lie with men."

"Oh." Finn thought about this for a moment. "Does that mean all incubuses are different?"

"Are all humans different?"

"Of course."

Tarric shrugged. "There you have it."

"So incubuses don't only like women, and they don't crush or suffocate people to death, and they don't force themselves on anyone?"

"Natural Law. We cannot force ourselves on any person unwilling, any more than you could sprout wings and fly. But even assuming such was possible, there would be little point. I cannot gain nourishment without desire. You humans feed on bread and water. Incubi feed on the appetites of the flesh. Human flesh, to be exact," Tarric finished, grinning again.

"So why would people write that?"

"I can only assume they haven't had much in the way of firsthand experience," Tarric said, disdain coloring his voice. "And if they're the kind of people to speak with authority on subjects they clearly know nothing about, I can certainly see why. Ugh." He shuddered in disgust at the thought. "As I said, we choose our so-called *victims*."

"Oh." Finn paused. "Does that mean . . ."

Tarric waited, looking at Finn now with something like amusement.

"Well, you chose Master Kestrall. Then you chose me. Are you . . . er . . ."

"Oh, you humans and your possessiveness," Tarric sighed, although he did not seem displeased at the question. "Always speaking of sex as though it's something that can be owned. But no, if you absolutely must know, I have not visited your master again since then, and will not. His need was fulfilled, and he is wise enough to know it. In any case, it's not advisable for my kind to form attachments. Natural Law exists for a reason."

"I see." Finn felt unaccountably relieved at this answer. "So there's no truth at all to anything that's been written about incubuses . . . incubi, I mean?"

"Oh, there are occasional glimmers of truth in old tales," Tarric said, clearly noticing Finn's continued interest. "If we are summoned by human effort rather than our own, there is a cost — as you yourself now know. But I know of nobody who's been driven mad by or died from it. Although, that's not to say there probably aren't plenty of people who try to summon things they shouldn't who are mad already," Tarric added, considering. "Personally, however, that's not at all to my taste. No, not at all." He made a face. "I'll stick to men with little in the way of arrogance but plenty of curiosity, thank you very much . . . and those who may lack knowledge, yet instinctively know exactly what they want."

Under his unabashed stare, Finn squirmed and flushed all over again. "*Do* people summon other beings often?" he asked, changing the subject.

"Often? I would say not. Such knowledge is not commonplace, and those that gain it do not often have the required . . . shall we say *talent*, for putting it to good use."

"What about demons? Do people summon them?"

Tarric stilled. There was a brief silence. " . . . I sincerely hope," the incubus said pointedly, "that you are not thinking of trying any such thing."

"Of course not! I was just . . . you know, curious."

"And thus far, your abundant curiosity has not landed you in too much trouble — although it could well have. Be wary," Tarric said, still uncharacteristically serious. "Only the foolhardiest of men, or those driven mad by their own need for power, would willfully summon a demon into their midst. Never does it end well for them."

The incubus flicked his hands as though to physically rid himself of the thought, and Finn was about to change the subject again when a yawn overtook him, stretching his mouth wide. His eyes felt suddenly heavy.

"You looked rather *dried out* yourself, my dear."

"Ha ha." Finn hesitated. "Are you . . . leaving?"

"I may not stay. I may be in human form now, but this is

not my true nature. I cannot exist here like this, with you, for long. It would quite literally kill us, in fact."

"But I'll see you again. You said three times."

"I said it was only possible thrice," Tarric corrected him.

"Natural Law?"

"Indeed."

"Then I won't waste my next chance." Finn gave no indication of his sinking disappointment at the words. He knew speaking of it wouldn't change anything, and it felt churlish to protest when Tarric had already done more for Finn than he probably knew.

Gentle laughter filled the small room. "Be assured, you did not waste this one. Now, close your eyes." Finn obeyed, even knowing Tarric was still looking at him—feeling the sensation of that gleaming gaze roving his body. Then Tarric spoke again, and now his voice held a tone of something akin to wonder. "I wonder why I am so protective of you, young apprentice. I know perfectly well I must go, and yet . . ."

Although Finn waited, the incubus did not finish the sentence. Instead, Finn felt the strangely gentle touch of a kiss at his temple, followed by the sound of a flame sizzling quietly out.

When he opened his eyes again, the chamber was dark once more and the incubus was gone.

The weeks passed, and although the weather continued long and hot, at night, the air began to hold a hint of coolness.

For Finn, the time seemed to pass abnormally slowly, his studies as well as the harvest celebration preparations with Kestrall continuing day by long day, until at last he was almost startled to realize the festival was finally upon them.

"I've hired another two young lads to help us carry everything," his master said, seated opposite Finn at the table in the kitchen the evening before the festivities. "We won't be bringing any other supplies with us—there's neither space nor privacy enough to make anything not already created."

Finn dutifully nodded. "Yes, Master Kestrall."

"But we are taking future orders. Be sure to take people's names and what they want down—and tell them where they can find the shop if they don't already know."

"Yes, Master Kestrall."

"And don't forget, offer to write the details down yourself if they prefer. Some wish for privacy and won't want to speak their needs aloud, but plenty won't be proficient in writing. Be as detailed as you can—but not intrusive."

"I know, Master Kestrall."

"Keep the list behind you where nobody can see it." The magician wrung his hands, as nervous as though their market stall would be the center of attention when, in reality, they would be squeezed between a scribe and a candle maker. "Oh, and if anyone asks for a fortune, send them across the way to the fortune-teller. Politely. We're not in the business of—"

"Master Kestrall, it's going to be *fine*. I already know all these things—you told me yesterday, and the day before that. Probably the one before that, too. I've lost count."

"You're right, of course." Kestrall made to push his eyeglasses further up his nose, realized he'd taken them off to polish them, and hastily looked around.

"Here." Finn handed him them from where they'd been lying on the other side of the table. "It's not really any different than normal. It's just our stock's been made beforehand and the shop has changed locations for the day, you said so yourself."

"Yes, well. Preparation is key to all things."

Finn followed his master's gaze around the kitchen. The table and benches around them were full—amulets and charms, designed to be either worn beneath clothing or placed at key points around the home or business, mixtures of herbs and oils, candles and stones in different colors and shapes and inscribed with various patterns or sigils. These had all been piled neatly into wicker baskets and would be laid out on trestle tables in accordance with their form and intent. Finn was to keep a surplus behind him and ensure that the tables remained well-stocked and presented, as well as to take money, write future orders, and provide the customers with instructions about how to use the magick most effectively.

Finn, who had helped create most of the charms alongside Kestrall over the past weeks, was satisfied with their work and not particularly worried about how the day's business would go. Kestrall was a well-respected and well-liked man among his neighbors and customers alike, after all, and as far as Finn knew, business had never been as high. If Finn was nervous at all, it was because he had never really acclimatized to being around so many people at once, especially for the full space of a day. His master, on the other hand, had been worrying and fretting over every detail of their festival day, and had made Finn wash himself thoroughly in the courtyard and scrub his clothes until the fabric had nearly begun to wear thin.

"Ask me if you're not sure about anything or if someone's being difficult. There are those who are less than friendly toward magicians, especially those of us making a living from it." *Especially the priests.* He did not say it, but it was common knowledge the priests did not approve of the likes of magicians and fortune-tellers, and never had. To them, magick came only from the gods, and their gifts were bestowed only on the faithful—magicians were therefore heretics and not to be trusted. Still, there had never been any trouble in this city that Finn was aware of, and for all they held positions of authority, no priest had the right to put a stop to any lawful business.

Finn sighed. "Yes, Master Kestrall."

A knock at the door forestalled whatever Kestrall was about to worry over next, and Finn rushed to answer it. "Sorry, we're closed for the — oh, Rosie."

"Evenin', Finn." Rosie looked a little nervous as she peered at him. "Evenin', sir," she added as Kestrall, recognizing the voice, came up behind Finn.

"Is everything all right, Rosie? Is it your ma? I thought she was doing better lately."

"Nah. I just came to talk to Finn for a bit, if that's all right with you, sir."

"Of course. Come in, sit down. You'll have some tea, yes? I just made a fresh pot."

Rosie hesitated, but Kestrall ushered her to the table and then busied himself clearing enough space for her to sit. Then, when Rosie looked around uncomfortably, he seemed to realize that she wanted a little privacy and turned away, bustling around the kitchen and leaving Finn and Rosie to their conversation.

"Ready for tomorrow?" Finn asked her.

"Oh, aye." Rosie fiddled with the lacing on her dress. "Ma's had me at the loom for *weeks*. I've barely left the house at all. Says we have to make up for all the time she weren't working on account of her back."

"She's doing well, then?"

"Aye, but only because she finally started drinking what the physicker gave her, though she still credits the charms for everything." Rose darted a glance at Kestrall. "No offense, sir."

"None taken, Rosie." Kestrall put down two gently steaming cups and retreated, muttering something about forgetting some supplies left in the basement. Finn scowled at his back, knowing his master had left no such thing, but unable to say so in front of Rosie.

"Pa says she's daft, but nobody's able to convince her otherwise."

"Aye, well . . . so long as she's better, that's what matters, I s'pose."

Rosie nodded and looked down. "Finn . . . actually, I came here to ask a favor. But I want it kept between us and all. If Ma finds out . . ." She looked at him entreatingly. "She already thinks I don't keep myself to myself enough. Every time I go out, she wants to know why, and I can't even have a moment's peace if I'm not working or helping around the house."

Finn nodded. "I'll not tell anyone. Not even Master Kestrall if you don't want."

Rosie gifted him with a grateful smile. "Thanks, Finn." She took a polite sip of her tea and leaned forward, and from her bobbing chestnut curls, Finn caught the strong scent of lily. "I knew I could count on you. Everyone's always saying so, even Ma."

"Go on, then," Finn said, uncomfortable now himself.

"It's just . . . well, I'll be kept busy the whole day tomorrow at Market Square and I was wondering if . . . I know they're marked for customers, but I'll pay and all!"

"Pay for what?" Finn asked, confused.

"A love charm," Rosie said half-defiantly, as though expecting her ma to storm in that very second and drag her out by the ear.

"For you, you mean?"

"It'd mean the world to me, Finn! Only I don't expect there to be any left by the time Ma lets me go, she'll keep me chained to the stall the entire day. So I was wondering if you could just . . . save one for me, like."

"Why don't you just ask for one from here like normal?" Finn asked, confused.

"'Cos it *has* to be tomorrow. *Please*, Finn! I can't ask for it tonight for fear Ma'll find out, she's always snooping about so. And if I don't get one tomorrow, it'll be too late. Ma will give me some coin tomorrow after business is done and I can pick the charm up from you. What do you say?"

Finn could think of no reason to refuse her, even if he still felt vaguely uneasy, though he couldn't put his finger on why. "All right."

"Thanks, Finn!" She looked as relieved as though she might be about to jump up and hug him, and Finn pushed his chair back hastily.

"It's no problem. I'll see you tomorrow then, yeah?"

"Aye!" Her eyes sparkled.

Finn cleared his throat. "Well then . . ."

"Oh!" Rosie hurriedly stood up. "Sorry for bothering you so late. I was trying to get away the entire day. I didn't mean to bother you or Master Kestrall, and right before the festival and all . . ."

"Nah." Finn stood awkwardly and waited until she'd gone, leaving her tea mostly untouched.

At the sound of the door squeaking closed behind her, Kestrall made his way noisily up the stairs. "All's well, then?" When Finn merely nodded, Kestrall cleared his throat. "If you want some time to yourself tomorrow evening, I'm sure that could be arranged."

"No!" Finn said hastily.

"Are you sure?" Kestrall looked at him searchingly. "I didn't overhear anything, mind, but Rosie sounded very . . . determined."

"She only wants to—er . . ." He'd been about to say *pick up a charm*, but remembered he'd promised not to mention it even to Kestrall, and trailed awkwardly off.

"Well, I think you'll have earned yourself some time off regardless," Kestrall decided for him. "Besides, I don't expect all the stock to sell—I've probably gone and made too much," he said, looking around at the multitude of baskets topped high with merchandise. "And once evening sets in, everyone will be busy with the drinking and dancing portion of the festival. If anything's left of ours, I can carry it back myself or find another lad to help me." He winked at Finn. "You come on back in your own time, yes?"

"I s'pose," Finn mumbled, not daring to say anything that might lead to the topic of Finn's preferred taste in bed partners.

"You're welcome," Kestrall said cheerily, clearly taking Finn's reticence for bashfulness over Rosie's attention. His earlier nervousness seemed to have miraculously disappeared for the moment. "Everything will work out as it should, you'll see."

Finn wasn't so sure. Even so, he reflected after a moment, perhaps it was as well that his master had allowed him some time alone tomorrow night.

He didn't know what he'd say to Rosie when the time came for her to admit her feelings for him — but the festival would give him the perfect opportunity to finally confess himself to Jonti.

CHAPTER EIGHT

The day of the harvest festival dawned clear and bright.
Finn was out of bed early, as was Kestrall, rubbing his
eyes, unaccustomed to the early hour. Whereas his master
had been nervous the day before, now he seemed perfectly
composed, sitting down to eat a simple breakfast of bread and
cheese without hurrying through his meal. In contrast, Finn
was far more on edge, though Kestrall made no comment at
the way he scoffed his food and stood up, brushing fussily at
his clothes.

Despite retiring to bed at an early hour, Finn had spent
much of the night awake and thinking about what exactly he
would say to Jonti when the time came, and where he would
say it. Should he go to the Crow's Nest after Kestrall told him
he was free to leave for the evening, Finn wondered again
now? But by then the book shop would be closed too, and
Jonti probably enjoying the festivities somewhere, maybe eating or attending one of the many street performances.

It would indeed be a crowd. The harvest festival attracted
entertainers from far and wide, offering plenty in the way of
amusement for the townsfolk, many of whom chose to stay
out most of the night. The older among them might not trudge
home until dawn, having finally eaten — and drunken — their
fill and sung, danced or cheered their friends on until they
were ready to collapse. Meanwhile, for shop keepers, tavern
owners, brewers, artisans, performers, pickpockets and
whores, it was one of the most lucrative days of the entire
year. While the more conservative townsfolk might decry the

festivities as excessive, even unholy—the priests especially had long since spoken out against it, though these protestations had always been roundly ignored, and the presence of the City Watch around Market Square would be conspicuous as always—it hadn't yet stopped anyone else from enjoying the celebrations to the fullest.

Even so, Finn reasoned, Jonti should not be too hard to find. There would surely be little reason for him to wander far from Market Square, where all of the main festivities took place, so Finn would just have to search until they bumped into one another.

As for what Finn would do then . . . well, Jonti was already aware of Finn's feelings, so how hard could it really be to find a place a little out of the way—a quiet pocket of privacy while Finn finally said what he'd kept hidden away inside for months? Jonti might have somewhere in mind already, or even—Finn felt himself grow hot at the very thought—spare him from making his confession with a kiss. Jonti wasn't shy, and he'd certainly never been stupidly clumsy or tongue-tied around Finn, so it stood to reason that he'd be simple and direct in his actions. Almost as much as . . .

Finn shook his head. Now was *not* the time to be thinking of Tarric. He was not human—they were clearly not meant to be together. *Jonti* was the one Finn belonged with. His eyes were a clear, uncomplicated blue, yes, and his hair was nearly as bright as the sun. He was not guarded, and he did not hold any magickal secrets or have any knowledge of any other world but this one. But he was handsome just the same, and no doubt still far cleverer than Finn would ever be, and Finn had always wanted to know more of him. Tonight, he finally would.

A sudden rapping sound made Finn jump. Kestrall calmly got up and opened the door while Finn pretended he hadn't just knocked his cup over.

"Mister? I'm Curly—I'm here to help fetch your things for Market Square. This here's my brother, Tam." The boy who spoke was young and snub-nosed, and looked delighted when Kestrall put some coppers into his hand upfront. The boy who stood silently beside him, a smaller version of Curly himself, craned his head to look, eyes wide.

"Good lads, you're nice and early. Follow me and make sure not to let anything spill on the ground, and you'll have the rest once we arrive, aye?"

Curly nodded eagerly.

The walk to Market Square was busy yet uneventful. As it was still too early for the festivities to have begun, it was mainly only tradesfolk and other stallholders organizing themselves and their wares for the day, plenty of time before the festivalgoers and most visitors to the city were even up. Finn scurried behind Kestrall, struggling to keep up with his longer strides, and the errand boy and his younger brother scurried to keep up with Finn, valiantly keeping any of the wares held in the oversized baskets from tipping out.

"Here we are." Kestrall looked behind him, looking vaguely surprised to see Finn as well as both Curly and Tam still some way behind him. The two youngest caught up at last, both breathing heavily, and Kestrall's expression grew sheepish. "Sorry, boys. And thank you, Curly, Tam. For your trouble, lads." An entire silver piece found its way into Curly's hand, and his eyes grew as round as the coin itself.

"Thanks, Mister," he whispered, and the boys quickly melted away, no doubt before they thought Kestrall might change his mind.

The festival organizers had clearly been at work since even earlier that morning, for most of the trestle tables had already been put in place, with those selling their wares from carts and wagons likewise in the midst of arriving and settling down. Colorful banners hung from nearby shops and were strung up on makeshift lines, fluttering a little in the wind. Finn looked at the empty tables standing before them.

"Right." Kestrall rubbed his hands together. "Look lively, Finn. We've magick to sell."

By midday, their stocks had already been much depleted.

Many of the more traditional charms and amulets had been the first to go, as well as those more popular with the younger folk—magick to bring money, promote good fortune, and of course, find love. The candles, too, were popular—most likely, Kestrall told Finn, because they usually came with no particular instructions and simply looked pretty, whereas many of the more powerful charms tended to be far plainer in appearance and weren't designed to sit on a table or window-sill but rather be kept more private.

Finn, knowing that Kestrall would not mind, especially since it would bring them no less profit for their work, quickly pilfered a love charm with no sense of guilt when Kestrall's back was turned, remembering how Rosie had begged him to say nothing. She had promised to find Finn later, and so he kept the charm safely out of sight in his pocket for now, thinking little more about it.

The day's business continued, the lines and sounds of excited customers seemingly never-ending. Finally, a brief lull in the crowd gave Kestrall and Finn each time to buy food enough to sustain their energy until evening. When his turn came, Finn bought a thick fish soup and a game pastry that scorched his tongue but was worth every flaky bite.

"All right, Finn?" his master asked when he'd made his way back to their table.

"Well enough." Finn had never been entirely comfortable around a lot of people at once, all making noise and jostling for attention, and even after these years spent as a lawfully hired apprentice, the heavy presence of the City Watch made him jumpy. Then again, Kestrall probably wasn't used to such crowds either, Finn reflected. Even so, his master had kept his composure throughout the day, dealing with each customer politely and allowing the little ones time to pore over the wares, while deftly answering the questions of the older customers.

"That's right, ma'am, just in the boy's crib will do, so long as you keep it somewhere close to his body—it doesn't need to be around his neck, the string is just for convenience." Kestrall sent away the woman who'd come for an amulet for her baby to guard against fever with a reassuring nod, then beckoned to the child standing quietly behind her, who wore an expression of open amazement.

"Are you really a magician, Mister?"

"I am indeed. What can I do for you, young lady?"

"Can I have this colorful one?"

The girl, barely the height of the table she peered over, reached out for a charm sewn with red and glittering gold-colored thread.

Kestrall hesitated. "You're a little young for that, I'm afraid," he said, plucking it gently from her hand. It was, Finn saw, an amulet to help prevent stomach upsets in women—something he himself knew little of and was more than happy to remain ignorant about.

The girl's face fell.

Kestrall cast a glance over the table. "You want something pretty, aye? Maybe something that'd look nice at home? Or do you want something to wear as a necklace?"

The girl considered. "A necklace please, Mister."

"Right you are. Finn, hand me the amulet edged in green, will you?" He showed it to the girl, who examined it curiously.

"What does this one do?"

"It brings good luck, especially for people who like to be

outside, or who travel a lot. You like to be outside, right?"

The girl's mouth opened wide. "How did you know?" she asked in an awed whisper.

Kestrall smiled and winked. "Magician's secret," he said.

"Is this enough?" She held out four copper coins.

"More than." Kestrall took three of them, even though Finn knew very well he usually charged five, and smiled again. "You don't have to wear it all the time, but if you go somewhere far, it will bring you extra luck. When the string breaks on its own, you can either burn it or bury it in the earth, and the luck will stay strong until you find time to get a new one."

The girl beamed. "Thanks, Mister!"

Finn sidled up to Kestrall once she'd disappeared back into the crowd at a jubilant run. "How *did* you know?" he asked quietly.

"There was plentiful dirt under her fingernails," he replied. "And by the looks of her clothes, she's from somewhere out in the countryside. Her family's likely farming folk."

Finn shook his head and went back to work. Truly, he thought, there was a lot to learn about being a good magician.

The afternoon drew on and trade began to slow further toward evening, until finally there were longer breaks between customers. Even the fortune-teller set up opposite them, who had been glaring at them all morning despite Kestrall sending several customers her way, looked pleased now that business was winding down. It had been a profitable day for all.

Kestrall looked up at the sky. His hair was mussed, the lines on his face more pronounced than they had been that morning. "I reckon it's time you can go now," he told Finn. "What stock we have left likely won't sell much more, and I'd like a bit of time to look around myself later, before all but the food carts pack up." He glanced longingly in the direction of the traveling peddler and his cart, which stood only a few paces away from the fortune-teller. The peddler was selling various trinkets from places afar, and Kestrall had no doubt seen the several books among his collection.

People were starting to drift toward makeshift stages, and in the distance, Finn heard the sound of drums being struck. The sky had just begun to darken, though the torches had not yet been lit. Finn hesitated. "Are you sure?"

Kestrall dug a few coins from his pocket and handed them to Finn, waving him away. "Go on, lad. Enjoy your youth!"

Finn scowled to cover his embarrassment and left, allowing the noise of the crowd to wash over him. Rosie had not yet come to pick up her charm, he realized, and he veered toward the stalls selling clothing, tapestries and other decorative fabrics.

It took him several minutes to push his way through the crowd, largely against the tide of people heading for the center of the square. Finally, he spotted Rosie's mother, looking red-faced and wiping her face of sweat with her apron.

"Mrs. Webb?"

"Young Finn! How's the master magician faring at his stall?"

"Well enough, Mrs. Webb, thank you. Are you finishing for the day?" Her stall, too, stood now largely empty of wares.

"Aye, thank the gods for that. My back's starting to act up again, it is."

"Have you seen Rosie about?"

"I was about to ask the very same! She was supposed to be back here an hour ago, the naughty thing! Too bold for her own good, is my Rosie. Her own pa can't control her even when I make him threaten her with his stick. Too lenient on her, he is, I'm forever telling him so . . ."

Not wanting to get Rosie into any more trouble, Finn simply bid her mother goodbye, figuring he might run into her while he was looking for Jonti. He drifted toward the stage, half-pulled along by the crowd, pausing once in a while to look over the wares left at the other stalls. Tantalizing smells greeted him, and his stomach growled. His master had been generous, and Finn had more than enough to buy food for the evening, even drink if he wished, though he only rarely took even an ale with dinner.

His neck prickled. Quickly, Finn stopped and looked around, not running to duck into a doorway as he once would have, but aware something didn't feel quite right. Still, he saw nobody watching him, and after a moment, tried to shake the feeling off, deciding it must simply be the day catching up with him. He wasn't used to being around so many people in such close proximity for hours on end, after all. Small wonder his nerves were a little on edge.

"Looking for hot food, Mister?" Finn jumped, but it was only a young lady from behind him, still a girl, really, who smiled and pointed a little way further down a narrow street leading off from the square. "My brother's still selling leek pottage. It has a bit of meat in it," she added temptingly.

Finn nodded, thanking her, and obligingly joined the line of people waiting to purchase the food, only a small handful of customers waiting to be served in front of him. He jingled his pockets and glanced about again, not really expecting to see anybody he knew.

A low laugh caught his attention.

Jonti.

Finn's heart gave a leap of surprise and anticipation, and in his other pocket, he fingered the love charm still there for Rosie. Well, maybe it was working for him, too, he thought a little giddily. He'd been the one to make it, after all. The laugh came again, and Finn left the line, his earlier hunger forgotten, walking in the direction he thought it'd come from.

"Jonti?" he called quietly.

There, just around the corner. A flash of sunny blond hair

caught his eye, and a murmured voice.

"Jonti!"

He rounded the next bend.

He stared.

He dropped the love charm from fingers gone suddenly numb.

He turned and ran, not wanting to see any more. Not wanting to be seen.

Not wanting to replay the image in his head, over and over again, of Rosie, her skirts gathered up around her waist, moaning softly as Jonti, his hands about her hips and his eyes closed in undisguised pleasure, fucked her against the wall.

Finn panted and looked about him. He'd simply run, not thinking to go anywhere in particular so long as it was away — from the crowd, from Jonti and Rosie, from Kestrall's probing questions, from everything. He felt suffocated, and though his eyes were dry and his feelings locked deep inside, his throat was raw. He supposed he was out of practice running.

He'd earned a few stares, a boy sprinting full tilt away from rather than toward the festivities, and a few people had yelled after him when he'd come close to colliding with them. Finally, he'd slowed to a walk, wandering aimlessly, his thoughts adrift. Now he was attracting a few strange looks again.

Finn looked down at himself, suddenly self-conscious. The docks were no place for gentlefolk with no clear business, and it stank of rotting fish and weed, of stale beer and piss. Though he was clearly no noble, still he was far too clean and well-dressed for such a place and time. The men out here now had pinched faces, and women were scarce. Those he did see walked closely alongside the men so that their bodies pressed together, their hair worn conspicuously loose. They were whores and doxies, Finn saw immediately, and began to recall his wits.

He turned back in the direction he'd come, though he quickly realized he didn't know what routes he'd taken to get here. He must have run a long way without knowing it, for the docks were situated a good distance from Market Square, crisscrossed in between by any number of poorly-lit streets and narrow alleyways, some with walls short enough to jump over and others that led to dead ends if you didn't know your way.

Head down, shoulders hunched in an effort to blend in better, Finn walked more slowly, knowing that running would only make him more noticeable. He hadn't returned here since Kestrall had taken him in, and for good reason—in the day it might be rough, but alone and at night, only a fool would stroll around these parts without purpose and with no form of protection, especially if they had coin in their pockets. Little had changed over the years in that regard.

Finn looked around and ducked into one of the many alleyways leading away from the water. The smell of fish gradually receded, although other smells grew stronger. Finn fought to keep from covering his nose—a dead giveaway. He heard shrill laughter coming from a nearby tavern, followed by angry shouting, and turned sharply left, away from the sound.

Now it was silent but for a persistent *drip, drip* of something that Finn had no urge to investigate. He continued to walk a while, silent and shivering a little now. He'd not brought his cloak.

Soon he stopped, goosebumps prickling his skin. Was he being followed? No, it must be only his imagination, old fears coming back to haunt him. He resumed his pace, allowing himself to move quicker, and now his heart leaped into his throat. He had definitely heard the soft patter of footsteps behind him. Whoever it was wore no shoes, of that he was certain—bare feet on hard stone. You never forgot some things.

He rounded another corner and stopped, hardly daring to breathe. If he was truly being followed, he could not see them, but that meant they could not see him either, he reasoned. In the rapidly dimming light, there was a good chance he could lose them if he was but quiet enough, even if they were faster and better knew their way around.

When Finn heard nothing more for at least a minute, he crept a few steps further, his ears sensitive to any sound that might break the silence. The soft footsteps from behind him moved too, and fresh sweat broke out over his body. He bolted, barely keeping from crashing into the walls as he darted from one alleyway to another, turning sharply left and right until he was gasping for air, his energy beginning to give out.

"Little Finny . . ."

Finn did not have time to yell. The last thing he glimpsed before the blow to the back of his skull made the world turn dark before his eyes was Jasom, his broken, jagged grin leering at him from out of the gloom.

CHAPTER NINE

The sound of his own body being dragged roughly over the ground tipped Finn into gradual awareness. His arms were stretched out over his head, and his head felt heavy and lolled back, occasionally scraping the stone beneath him. His tongue was dry and glued to the top of his mouth. He tried to speak, coughed, and kicked out feebly.

Jasom looked back at him from where he and another boy Finn only vaguely recognized were hauling him by the wrists. "Awake, little Finny?"

Groggily, Finn raised his head further and looked about him. It was dark now—night had truly fallen and there was nobody about. "What—"

"Don't scream, or I'll break your wrists," Jasom warned. Then he grinned. "Been watching you all day, I have. Never thought you'd make your way to this side of town all by yourself, though. Made my job far easier, that."

Finn shivered, trying to hide his sudden rush of fear by glaring at his captor instead. "Where the fuck are you taking me?"

Jasom shrugged. "Find out soon enough, won't you?" His companion only sniggered.

Finn began to struggle, trying to wriggle his wrists free and dig his feet into the ground, but he could find no purchase, and Jasom grinned down at him again, revealing a mouth with gaping holes where some of his teeth should have been. "Enough of that. Besides, I only get half coin if I bring you *too* damaged."

Finn sniffed. "My compliments to whoever did that to your face," he said. "I should send them a thank-you note."

In response, Jasom nodded to his companion, who released Finn's other wrist, leaned down, and dealt him such a blow that his sight dimmed again and his ears rang. For several minutes, the world spun sickeningly, and Finn grew limp as he was dragged onward, the pain in his head receding to the back of his mind.

At some point, he caught snatches of conversation being spoken into the gloom. " . . . Said *two* silver pieces, not one."

" . . . Already drawn blood," a man said in reply.

" . . . And how was I s'posed to . . . could have been seen as I dragged him across the whole bloody town . . . one fuckin' silver!"

A long pause, followed by a sigh. " . . . The church . . . for your work. May the gods bless you."

When he could no longer feel the ground beneath him, the cold seeping through his shirt, Finn knew someone had hauled him up and was carrying him, this time somewhere inside. The air was thick and heavy with the smell of smoke and incense, and Finn peered groggily up, aware that whoever held him was far taller than he, older and bearded, the flicker of numerous candles reflecting from half-moon eyeglasses.

Finn's body gave a jerk of recognition. Where had he seen this man before? The stranger tutted but didn't speak, continuing to walk through the building until he placed Finn on top of some kind of wooden platform, roughly the same length as his body. When Finn struggled to sit up, feeling the taught stretching of dried blood caked on the back of his scalp, the man bound his wrists and then his feet, his movements efficient and business-like.

"What . . . what are you . . ." The words slipped from his mouth so thickly that he wondered if he'd been drugged.

The man looked at him, not frowning, not smiling. "Be silent, magician's apprentice."

"The . . . the *fuck* are you—"

"You shall not sully this place with your foul mouth!" the man warned, more sternly now.

Finn screamed then, knowing where he was, hoping someone nearby might hear him, but his cry was weak, and the sound of his voice only echoed a little and crashed back down at him from the high beamed ceilings.

"Scream all you like," said the priest, for that was surely what he was. His black robes hid most of his body, but Finn could see he looked old and reedy, his face sunken and his skin sallow, though his voice held a note of unmistakable authority. They'd passed each other by in the street, Finn recalled, too late now to do anything about it. "It grows late, and the revelers are far from the sanctity of this holy place. I watch the church alone tonight as my brothers in faith pray for those lost souls wandering the streets, abusing their bodies with drink and with one another. Nobody will come for you."

"What have . . . you done to me? What are you . . ."

"Be silent," the priest told him again, and began circling the platform widdershins, chanting something in a strange language under his breath and leaving Finn to gather his wits and regain control of his speech.

"Hey. Hey, priest. Priest!" he called, trying to disrupt the man from whatever he thought he was doing. "Shut up for a minute and listen to me. My master knows I'm here."

At that, the priest left off chanting. "Your master," he said, and looked angry for the first time. "Your master is a twisted soul. He took you in, an innocent boy, and corrupted your spirit. Now I must exorcise your demons before they have the chance to poison you completely."

"You're crazy. You think I'm possessed?"

"I know it. My gods will drive the demons from your body, using my own as a tool for their divine works."

Finn grew colder at these words. He tried again, more desperately now. "Master Kestrall will know something's wrong. So will my friends. They'll find you and have the Watch on you for what you're doing! Paying people to kidnap folk, tying them up . . . priest or not, you'll be imprisoned." He was bluffing, knowing that Kestrall thought he was with Rosie and would not grow worried until Finn failed to appear by the morning.

"They will do no such thing," the priest replied calmly. "Nobody knows you are here. However, your master is known to *me*. No doubt he is still peddling his profane wares to the poor, unsuspecting public. Such blatant wickedness ought not to be tolerated. Yet if I can save even one soul from a man such as he — a sorcerer meddling with dark forces to satisfy his own hunger for power — that knowledge is reward enough."

At this unlikely description of the same man who'd taken Finn from the street and given him a home and a trade, Finn actually laughed, despite the situation. "Priest, you have no idea what you're talking about."

The priest ignored this and picked up his chant again, moving slowly around the platform. As he did so, he lit more candles, stopping before each one and raising his arms, imploring, invoking.

Finn recognized the same gesture from his own work with Kestrall and scoffed loudly, trying not to let his rising panic show. Whether he knew it or not, the priest wasn't about to exorcise anything. He was about to *summon* something.

"Hey. Hey, horse-face!" Finn tried again, more desperately now. "Your little spell isn't going to work."

"Spell!" The priest rounded on him. "I do not consort with black powers, but communicate with the gods!"

"I'm pretty sure your gods wouldn't look kindly on kidnapping," Finn snapped back. "Though a fucking *demon* might! Too bad for you you've no idea what you're doing—try drawing a magick circle next time, you two-bit magician."

"You dare!" The priest shrieked and raised his hands, this time to deal several blows to Finn's face, whipping his head back and forth. Finn bit his tongue and felt the blood trickle down his chin. At the sight of this, the priest abruptly stopped, his face eerily calm again, his eyes glittering with religious fervor.

He was mad, Finn decided, touched in the head. Whatever the old priest thought he was doing, he was clearly meddling in something far more dangerous than he comprehended.

"I do dare." Finn spat, accurately. "You're bent, as twisted as your beliefs. You think the gods will actually bless you for doing this?"

The priest wiped his cheek. "The possessed are often driven to acts of depravity and violence," he noted.

"*I'm* violent?" Finn demanded, incredulous.

"The demons inside you must be subdued. Yet that alone is not enough to drive them from your body. Divine intervention is the only answer to possession."

"I'm not possessed, you sadistic fucker!" Finn screamed again, twisting and jerking, his bound limbs thrashing as he swore every oath he could think of, raining down curses on his captor until his throat was raw and his body exhausted. Finally, he fell back, panting, tears of pure rage running down his cheeks, unable to move further.

Through it all, the priest stood silent, only holding Finn down so that he would not topple off the platform. Now he moved to rip Finn's shirt, letting the ragged ends fall open and exposing Finn's chest. "I see you are further gone than even I thought," he said, his voice grave. "You are raving, knowing not what you speak. We must begin immediately."

"No . . ." Finn whimpered as the priest placed his fingers on Finn's chin, wiping so that he collected some of the blood on his fingers. With this, he anointed Finn's chest, whispering something Finn didn't understand, his fingers moving from breastbone to navel.

"Stop . . . let me go . . ." Finn struggled feebly, but he had little more energy to give, and the older man clearly knew it.

Next, the priest moved down and removed Finn's shoes, allowing them to thump to the floor. He placed his hands around Finn's hips and jerked, ripping at the lacing and pulling down until Finn was all but naked, only his rent shirt now covering his shoulders and part of his sides.

Fear made Finn gulp for air as the priest made another circle of the platform, chanting again, making odd signs above Finn's head as he passed. Panic sought to rob Finn of his senses — the priest might not have been drawing a magick circle, but he was certainly walking one, and that might be enough if accompanied by the right words . . . or the right sacrifice.

Finn twisted his wrists around, then his ankles, hoping against hope that his bonds would give, even just enough to free one limb or to allow enough movement to defend himself. The leather remained stubbornly tight.

"Confess," the priest rounded on him suddenly. "Tell me of your past deeds, and of what was done to you against your will."

"The only thing being done against my will is this!" Finn would have spat again if he'd had saliva to spare. As it was, the dribble simply ran down his chin, mingling with the blood already there.

"Confess!" The priest seized his face, one hand on each cheek, forcing Finn to gaze straight up.

"You're the only demon here," Finn whispered, and the priest let him go, his head thumping back onto the hard platform. Finn groaned in pain, his skull pounding savagely.

"I see there is no choice." The priest began to disrobe until he stood bare to the waist. Then he resumed his chanting, swiping at Finn's chin again and anointing his own chest with the same blood he had smeared over Finn's stomach, painting a sigil on his skin Finn did not recognize.

The candles leaped, shadows dancing crazily on the walls. A foul stench filled the air, and the priest closed his eyes and lifted his arms and head toward the sky. "Ento mi yefel ofsendan, bogra oyrs . . ."

In sheer desperation now, Finn flailed again. "Help!" he cried with all the air left in his lungs. "Help me!" And then, with one last spurt of energy, he lifted his head and screamed the one name he could think of, and the one name he did not want to, knowing it could well be the last time—his throat tearing with the force of it, tasting the blood, warm and coppery, in his mouth.

"*Tarric!*"

For the space of a heartbeat, nothing happened.

Then the world erupted into light and fire.

The candles sputtered and sizzled, great globs of wax melting in an instant as the flames reared up, their tiny points becoming suddenly towering in size. The priest gave a shriek and covered his eyes, and Finn instinctively shielded his face at the blinding brightness.

When he moved his arms away, the priest was all but silent, choking, his feet scrabbling in the air for purchase. Tarric—Finn recognized him immediately, despite his monstrous height, despite the horns crowning his head and the fangs protruding from his mouth—held the priest above the ground, one hand encircling his neck. Long, curved, black claws caressed the priest's face.

"And you'd have the audacity to call *me* a demon," Tarric spoke. The sheer fury contained in these words, whispered as they were, made even Finn shudder.

The priest looked petrified, his mouth moving silently, either too afraid or simply held too tightly to respond. Tarric shook him, as easily as a ragdoll. "Well, priest? *Confess.*" This last word was spoken in a quiet hiss, mirroring the noise of the melting candles around them.

"I . . . I . . ."

Tarric snarled, an inhuman sound, and the flames danced wildly. "*You, you.*" He dug his claws deeper into the priest's flesh. "You are an insignificant husk, forsaken by all the gods. None of them will lift a finger to save you from the likes of *me.*" He shook the priest again, the man's limbs flopping uselessly, his head whipping back and forth. "Try to summon a demon, will you? I should perhaps thank you for your unholy desires. Your rampant greed, after all, is what helped guide me here when I was called . . . though certainly not by *you.*" His lips twisted in disgust. Thick, black liquid oozed from his deformed mouth.

The priest recovered wits enough to finally speak. "Beast," he said, numbly. "Hell-spawn."

"As you wish." Tarric roared then, loud and long, and the priest tried and failed to block his ears, the sound of his own scream lost to the noise.

When Tarric finally fell silent, the priest hung limp, his eyes closed.

"Tarric . . ." Finn spoke into the ringing silence. "Tarric, is he dead?"

Tarric turned to face him, and though his teeth were still fanged and dripping, Finn was not afraid. The incubus released his grip, the priest thumping to the ground where he lay, completely still.

"Unfortunately not. Unbeknownst to this so-called priest here, it is not within my power to kill him, or even do him serious harm . . . much as I would like that." Tarric glared down at the body splayed at his feet. "No, this one is not worth more of this, however much it would please me. He has seen enough—enough to either babble to his fellow priests and be considered a madman, put away for the rest of his days, or live them out in terror until finally his paranoia breaks his mind and he truly is driven mad by the demons of his own making." Tarric gave the body an experimental kick, but the priest did not move.

"Good." Finn struggled into a sitting position, wriggling over onto his stomach and using his hands to push himself upright, his own body feeling bruised and battered. "That creep deserves no less."

Tarric approached the platform, moving his hands through the air in a motion akin to slicing, and Finn's wrists and ankles were immediately released, his bonds falling away as neatly as though they had indeed been sliced through. He chafed at his skin, rubbed raw by the leather. "I didn't know you could do that."

"There is much I am capable of doing if I must. It is not for humans to know." Tarric leveled another glare at the prone form of the priest, then turned his gaze back toward Finn. "Are you all right?" He regarded Finn's chest, scowled fiercely, and passed his hand over the blood-smeared sigil, muttering something under his breath. The mark disappeared as though it had never been.

Finn looked at Tarric. He reached up, unhesitant, to feel the horns appearing from the incubus' hair. He knew him. He would always know him. "Yes," he said. "I'm all right. But you'd better put those away now. I don't think it'd be a good idea to let anyone else see them." He laughed shakily.

"Ah. Yes." They stared at one another, Tarric seeming to shrink in height as the light flickered over his face. His horns and claws retracted, his teeth flattening out and growing lighter. The black ooze disappeared as though it, too, had never existed—this only an illusion, like the rest of his form, Finn realized. Finally, the incubus snapped his jaw shut, feeling it over with one hand as though to check he'd done the job properly.

"I missed you," Finn said, and though he still felt angry that the priest had robbed him of more time—he hadn't been *ready* to call for Tarric, not yet, gods, not yet—he knew it was no good regretting. If Finn had not called for him, it could well have been too late for anything at all. You could not call for someone if you were dead.

As though thinking similar thoughts, Tarric moved his gaze slowly over Finn, taking in his bared form, the candlelight moving over his skin. The frown eased. The look in his eyes changed.

"I was going to say you should put your clothes back on," he said, his voice tickling over Finn and making him shiver, this time not with cold. "But on second thought, keep them off."

Finn panted, a few droplets of sweat rolling over his back and from under his arms, gliding down and pattering onto Tarric's chest. The incubus stared up at him, his back pressed to the floor and his eyes a burning, glittering green. His hands caressed Finn's hips and then slid further down, his fingers spread.

"Truly, you are a sight to behold," he breathed.

Finn shook his head and didn't reply. He didn't know if he could. All he knew was that a strange energy had taken hold of him, making his body throb not in pain but in anticipation and his cock go hard. There was no time to waste, and waste it he would not. He'd stood up, grabbed Tarric's hand and pulled—not that Tarric made any move to stop him—and they had dragged one another further back into the church until they found a small room, empty but for drawers full of candles and a few decorative holders and vases. Tarric had spoken a single word Finn did not understand, lighting the candles nearest the door, and without further speech allowed Finn to practically shove him to the ground.

Now they rutted, Finn atop the incubus, straddling the incubus' waist, his hands braced on Tarric's shoulders. He moved up and down, unashamed at the sounds their bodies made, slick and wet. He no longer cared for anything but this. Tarric's cock moved in and out, rubbing deliciously against Finn's insides. It jumped and quivered, especially when Finn wiggled his hips, drawing out long groans and appreciative sighs.

He didn't understand what had come over him and he didn't care. Call it relief, call it desire, call it magick—it didn't matter, he wanted only *Tarric*, wanted Tarric to want only *him* in return, and he allowed his body to be taken over with his longing, letting it do whatever it wanted, not attempting to mask his own strangled moans.

"This . . . this is . . ."

"Your third and final lesson," Tarric gasped. His eyes fluttered closed as he let out another low cry. "Need is not always about power or control," he continued, gasping a little. "Between lovers, need can cast out pain, banish exhaustion, drive the body solely on its own hunger, if only temporarily. And that is not always a bad thing, or cause for shame. Allow it to course through you . . ." He shuddered, his fingers tightening their hold. " . . . And channel it in the best way your body knows. And it will always know . . ."

Finn moved faster now, and his breath came hard and raw until it was almost a sob. He did not want this to end, but he felt the energy in him gathering into a ball, tight and low in his chest, and then expand outward until he thought his body might fly apart the same way his mind already had. His cock gave a jerk. He grabbed at it, pumping helplessly, spine curling in on itself, his thighs cramping as he continued to move frantically up and down. He might have let out a scream.

Tarric held him as he convulsed, his seed spurting forth, hot and viscous, the incubus' hands digging into his flesh, marking him as his cum filled Finn's hole.

Finn collapsed, his cock continuing to twitch as the shock and relief of what he'd done rolled over him.

"Shh, shh, it's all right, let it all out now, don't try to stop it . . ."

Finn felt the cum begin to drip down the backs of his thighs and the tears down his cheeks, and he shook his head. He felt no guilt, and little sadness despite the tears. He scarcely knew why he was crying, feeling only a numb kind of surprise. His ears were ringing again, in a heavy silence broken only by the equal heaviness of their breathing.

The incubus continued to hold him, his arms encircling Finn's back, his head resting on Finn's shoulder. He allowed Finn's breathing to quiet before he spoke again.

"Finn. Finn, wake up."

"I'm not asleep," Finn said, although he didn't remember closing his eyes and had no notion of how much time had passed.

"Good. You have to get up. We must leave this place."

Finn groaned. He didn't want to move. The sweat was making his body clammy, but he *ached*, as fiercely as though he'd been beaten from head to toe. Then he remembered he all but had been.

"Come. Your clothes. You cannot walk the streets naked."

"Ugh." His shirt was ripped, his trousers frayed, the lacing torn. Even so, the incubus would not let him rest, and bullied him into pulling on his clothes. "My shoes . . ." he remembered, but Tarric shook his head.

"No time. We have to leave, now."

"Why, what's going on?" Finn's head felt stupid and thick.

"*Time,*" the incubus said again, a little desperately. "You cannot find your way on your own in your current state. If I'm to get you back safely, it must be now."

Finn barely registered Tarric hauling him to his feet, or the feel of the incubus' hand on the small of his back, guiding Finn through a series of narrow corridors and small doors. He was more or less completely blind in the dark, for Tarric held no candle, but he either instinctively knew the way or could see perfectly well in the dark. Finn simply allowed himself to trust without fear of meeting anyone or hitting anything until finally, they emerged outside.

The cool air, free of the smell of wax or incense, awakened Finn's senses a little, and he shivered, pulling the two ragged halves of his shirt together over his chest. The moon was still high in the sky — for all an eternity might have passed since Finn had fled Market Square, little time had truly passed. He doubted the midnight bell had even been struck.

"This way."

They walked as quickly as they might, Finn shivering in earnest now, the shock catching up with him, and Tarric urged him on, half-pulling him through the largely abandoned streets. He steered them clear of people when they grew closer to the ongoing festivities, darting past doorways that spilled light and the sounds of laughter and merriment onto the cobblestones. Nobody paid them any mind, two dark shapes slipping through the only slightly lighter darkness of the city. They probably looked drunk, Finn thought.

Finally, recognizing the street they were on, Finn lifted his head tiredly. He pointed a finger, although Tarric clearly needed no guidance, and the incubus led them on, not through Market Square but around it, until they eventually stopped only a few more moments from Kestrall's door. Finn leaned weakly on Tarric for support.

"Here I must leave you," the incubus said. His face looked pinched, like he was in pain, or trying to hold it back.

"Don't." Finn knew before the word left his mouth that it was no use.

Tarric voice was hollow with regret. "I wish I could stay."

"Natural Law," said Finn dully.

"Yes."

"You would truly die?"

"We both would."

"Fuck your laws, then. Fuck them all. I love—"

Tarric stopped his words with a kiss, his tongue probing Finn's mouth, his hands running through Finn's hair and down his back. They kissed until Finn thought he might faint, his heart pounding and his chest begging for air. They kissed until their time ran out.

When his body was on the verge of collapse, when Finn finally shoved himself back out of necessity and opened his mouth to breathe again, he forced streaming eyes open, already knowing what he would see—and what he would not.

The space in front of him was empty. Tarric was gone.

Tarric was gone.

Finn tottered the rest of the way home, wanting to scream but knowing he could barely walk upright. The door was not barred. He forced it open and found Kestrall sitting at the table, surprise painted on his features as Finn stumbled inside.

"Finn? What's wrong, what's happened? Gods, you're bleeding, what on earth—"

Finn shook his head. "I fell," he said, his lips barely moving. "I fell and I hit my head."

"Are you drunk?"

"No . . . yes," Finn amended. Better his master thought that than anything else. "I just forgot." He pushed past Kestrall and down the hall, bumping against the wall several times, his sense of balance abandoning him. He shoved the door to his chamber closed behind him, not caring if Kestrall was following. He needed to lie down.

"Sorry," he muttered to nobody in particular. "Sorry . . ."

He fell into sleep almost instantly, his stomach pressed against the bed, his head buried in the pillow, as the truth seeped into his bones.

He would never see Tarric again.

CHAPTER TEN

"I heard what happened from Rosie's ma."

Finn was seated at the table across from his master as they quietly pieced together the correct ingredients for those charms and amulets they had received orders for during the harvest festival, a steaming pot of tea between them. Their shop door was shut, as was most other tradespeople's in the city. The two days following the festival were considered by most to be an unofficial holiday, allowing time enough for people to tidy, restock supplies, nurse hangovers, and in general take a well-earned rest after the whirlwind of activity.

Finn had remained in his room the entire previous day, nursing his various hurts, getting up only to attend to his body's needs. Mercifully, Kestrall had not asked him many questions, sensing Finn's need to be left alone. He had examined Finn's head, declared the wound not serious enough for the physicker to be called, and let Finn stew on his own in his bedchamber, neither calling him to do any work nor requiring him to speak. On the second day, as afternoon melted into evening, Finn finally made himself get up, eat a silent meal at the table, and work alongside his master as though nothing had happened.

Finn looked up at Kestrall's carefully neutral comment, grunting in acknowledgment. It would be the talk of the neighborhood, he knew. Jonti and Rosie had eloped, and neither of them had been seen by anyone since the evening of the festival.

"Did you see her before she . . . left?" Kestrall asked

delicately.

Mutely, Finn shook his head. Let Kestrall think he was pining after Rosie if he wanted. In truth, he'd given barely any thought even to Jonti, let alone Rosie.

Finn knew now that he had not loved him. After all, he had barely even known Jonti. Their interactions, he had realized while cooped up in his bedchamber, had been limited to a few incidental conversations and, on Finn's side at least, the pull of physical attraction. Jonti had likely never felt anything for Finn aside from a casual friendship. Finn's shock at seeing Jonti together with Rosie, his resulting flight nearly halfway across the width of the city, had been mostly out of hurt and embarrassment that Finn had mistaken Jonti's perfectly ordinary friendliness for something more. In reality, what Finn had thought to be love was only infatuation, which in any case had been gradually fading once the incubus . . . once Tarric . . .

Finn shook his head again to try and rid himself of the thought. Tarric wasn't coming back. He couldn't, even if he wanted to. *"No matter what I may wish, no matter how much you may desire, I can appear before you only thrice. That is not something in my power to alter."* Finn had played those words over and over in his mind until his head swam. Tarric would not lie — perhaps did not even have the ability to do so. No, he was gone from Finn's life now, never to return.

Finn concentrated on his hands twisting the fabric of his current amulet into the correct knots. Not a love charm, thank the gods — tactfully, Kestrall had not pushed any of those ingredients to his side of the table.

"There'll be another," the magician said, his voice gentle. "Give it time."

Finn had nothing but time now. He didn't want to think about the future, stretching out empty before him. He finished knotting the thread, bit the end off and pushed the amulet to the middle of the table. "The one for seasickness is done." He consulted the piece of parchment next to him and pulled the jar of lavender closer. "I'm starting on one to prevent headaches."

Kestrall nodded, waiting until Finn had settled to his task before speaking again. "It's all right to feel pain, you know. You lost something. Even if Rosie didn't love you in return, you loved her. There's nothing wrong in missing her."

"I know." He might have had only gotten to know Tarric over the span of several weeks, but his encounters had been far more meaningful than all of those with Jonti combined. Somewhere deep down, he'd known that. His experiences with Tarric, while unabashedly sexual in nature, had been no less genuine for all that. If anything, they'd been more honest, and certainly more real.

"Her mother's furious, of course," Kestrall said, perhaps trying to inject a little light-heartedness into the situation. "Says she'll get Rosie's pa to beat the girl black and blue if she ever comes back home." He smiled wryly. Rosie's ma was all bark and no bite, everyone knew that, although Rosie had no doubt received more than her fair share of tongue lashings.

"Aye, well."

"Try not to be too hard on the lass," Kestrall continued. "She probably felt trapped, caring for her mother all the time as she did and getting naught but temper back in return. It was plain to see the life of a weaver was not the one she would have wished for herself. Perhaps she chose freedom more than she really did Jonti, though no doubt the boy was more than willing."

"Maybe so," Finn said. He felt no anger at Rosie, who he had known for years but never been close to, and none for Jonti either, come to that. It was probably for the best.

"Of course, now that Jonti's gone too, the master bookkeeper at the Crow's Nest is none too pleased. He'll have to find another apprentice. One with less of an eye for the ladies."

Finn felt a reluctant smile tugging at his mouth. "Aye."

"There's few good lads around who know how to read well. He'd probably poach you if I let him."

"I'm not going anywhere." Finn finished measuring out the lavender and glanced around for the wormwood. "This is my home."

Kestrall pushed across the jar and patted him on the shoulder. "There's a good lad," he said.

The days turned into weeks, the weeks to months.

By day, little enough had changed. Finn kept the kitchen clean, sweeping the floors, scrubbing the table and valiantly doing his best to keep the clutter from building up to an uncontrollable degree. He still kept an eye on their main stock and ran errands for Kestrall, but more often now he studied out of books, practiced writing unfamiliar symbols and sigils, watched as his master instructed him in the creation of new charms and talismans, and tried his hand at creating them himself.

Now, however, a few of the ingredients he used required close supervision before Kestrall would trust them in Finn's hands by himself — some required extremely precise measuring or were unsafe if handled incorrectly, while others were exceedingly rare, or needed to be gathered in certain ways or at precise times to be of use at all. Many were not items that could be easily bought at an apothecary, or were difficult or expensive to source, and Finn learned that Kestrall had held on to some of these ingredients for years, carefully storing them away for times of need.

"Monkshood," said Kestrall, holding up a jar one evening. The leaves were dark, the dried petals a light purple. "Safe to touch, but poisonous to ingest. Used very occasionally for medicinal purposes, and when we use it in magick, it's usually to ward off very specific skin conditions, or sometimes to repel physical danger while on the road. Tinkers often carry it for this reason."

Finn nodded. "What about this one?"

"Kudu." The pink of the petals faded gradually to a shade that was almost white. "Pretty, but take care not to touch them with your bare skin, even when dried. The sap of the plant is poisonous enough to kill even larger animals if it gets into the bloodstream. However, when combined the right way with certain other herbs, it can be used as an effective charm to induce labor in women when the babies are trapped in the womb."

Finn nodded his understanding and held up another jar, far tinier than the rest, examining the contents. "This is bessomy, isn't it? I read about this in a book. It didn't say anything about being poisonous though."

"No. But the plant blossoms only rarely, and when it does, the flowers must only be gathered under the new moon for the magick to work. People have written about the plant as bringing good luck, but it would be more accurate to say it guards against bad — in particular, curses and other forms of evil that cannot be seen with the eye."

"And this is fumitory, I know." Finn hesitated. "It can also be used to guard against bad luck, right?" He avoided Kestrall's gaze.

"Yes, but it cannot be used on its own, and unlike most other herbs, it should not be burned, at least not for long. Breathe in the smoke and you'll soon go into convulsions and likely die without intervention. Magicians sometimes use it for protection when performing summonings. While not particularly rare, it should not be used lightly. Now." Kestrall got up, searched the shelves, and returned to the table with a slender book, handsomely embossed in dark red leather. "This book contains information on all of these plants and more. I was lucky enough to find it in reasonable condition some years ago. Be sure to read it carefully."

When Finn went to bed that night, the book tucked under his arm, he did not begin to read immediately. He stroked the cover. It reminded him painfully of Tarric.

Later on, his body bared to the darkness, he stroked himself to trembling release, mouthing Tarric's name helplessly. The incubus did not appear, nor did Finn expect him to, although that did not stop the sharp disappointment that came after., Neither did it stop Finn from pleasuring himself over many of the nights that followed, sometimes slowly, gradually, sometimes with a desperateness that shook him. Each time, rather than making the loss of Tarric easier to bear, the memories seemed to grow only more vivid. He filled Finn's mind, and Finn continued to grieve for what might have been, had the incubus not been bound to laws beyond Finn's understanding, and which Finn still cursed bitterly.

He did not know how to move on, however much Kestrall urged him to open his mind to other possibilities, and he did not know if he wished to. It would have meant losing the only thing Finn had left of Tarric, and this was something he could not bear to do.

Winter arrived suddenly. One minute the air still held a suggestion of warmth, and the next morning, a fine dusting of snow carpeted the ground. Now it lay everywhere, thick and heavy.

Finn walked briskly, his hands in his pockets, his ears burning, toward the Crow's Nest, another list of books in his hand that Kestrall had ordered from the master bookkeeper. The ground crunched beneath his booted feet and his breath was white on the air. Even the Watch was not out this bitterly cold day.

The bell over the shop jangled a welcome.

"Be right there, aye!" In a moment the master bookkeeper came bustling out, ink stains on his hands and dust on his apron as usual. "All right, Finn?"

Finn nodded. "Master Kestrall said you've his order ready?"

"That I do. Only five this time—lucky you," he grinned. "I've been keeping them out back. Mind, I should've sent my new assistant to deliver them so he could introduce himself. Right clever lad, he is."

Finn nodded again politely. The master bookkeeper would never take in someone he thought couldn't do the job—he was a fair man, but worked his apprentices hard and didn't tolerate slowness.

"Mind, I don't know where he showed up from, especially in this weather. Not much in the way of travelers coming in at all after the harvest is done, but he turned up here the other day as natural as can be, saying he wanted a job. And with only the clothes on his back!" The master bookkeeper tutted. "Says he's got no family and would take anyone who'd hire him. Wait a moment." He disappeared into the back room, and Finn heard the heavy thump of books being moved around. He winced, hoping they'd not be too heavy.

"Here you are, lad. Not too hard to find, most undamaged. Six silvers, nine coppers for the lot." He waited while Finn counted out the coins. "I was skeptical at first, I admit," he continued. "What boy comes to a book shop long after the snow's set in, asking for a job out of nowhere? But I'll admit, he can read and write like he was born to it, though he says his family was nobody of importance. Foreign-born, or so he claims. But a man's business is his own—so long as he does the job right, I'll not ask too many questions. Educated lads not too proud to work are hard to come by. You'll be wanting to meet him, aye?"

"Sure." Truthfully, Finn had little interest in whoever the

bookkeeper's new apprentice was, but he could hardly refuse the invitation.

The master bookkeeper turned behind him. "Boy!" he called. "Put down that manuscript—we'll sort those later, there's a whole pile as needs examining. Come meet one of our most frequent customers."

The apprentice bookkeeper emerged from the back room, walking smoothly around the desk against which his master leaned.

Finn dropped the list of books he'd been about to check. It fluttered soundlessly to the ground, and pale, slender fingers picked it up for him.

The young man's hair was pitch black, although bound tidily behind his neck by a simple strip of leather. He had a long face, sharply angled, and a mouth almost too wide for his narrow features. His skin was merely fair, not dramatically pale, and his narrow eyes, a bright, brilliant green, were entirely human.

Even so, no matter his form, Finn would have known him anywhere. He would always know him.

"Hello," said Finn, huskily.

Tarric smiled.

YOU MAY ALSO ENJOY THE FOLLOWING FROM EXTASY BOOKS INC:

Kaidyn's Courage
Diana Waters

Excerpt

Kaidyn was running.

Boots thumping on the uneven cobblestones, he darted around townspeople. He ran past rows of street merchants loudly hawking their wares, a band of children playing games with small colored stones, a pair of squabbling old women.

A hunk of meat was roasting on a spit, its owner trying—and failing—to keep the flies away. A small gang of sharp-eyed boys watched passersby, perhaps on the lookout for a rich pocket to pick, while a group of heavily bearded men threw cards at a rickety table. Nearby, a baby wailed in the arms of a woman who might have been its mother or its sister, attempting in vain to quiet it.

Not a drop of rain had fallen in weeks, and the earth was dry as a bone. Swirling dust and dirt and gods knew what else made Kaidyn want to shield his mouth. All the surrounding sights, smells, and sounds enveloped him, swallowing him up until he was just one of many, vanishing in the swarm of bodies.

Somewhere in front and a little to the right of him, Luck let out an exuberant whoop as though he was running a race instead of running from his superiors. "Lost 'em, Kai!" he shouted above the din. He slowed around the next corner and Kaidyn caught up to walk alongside him, eventually stopping to lean up against the shade of a twisted door frame. Luck thumped down beside him, grinning. "Told you it would work."

Kaidyn felt the corners of his mouth tilt upwards in response despite himself. "You did," he agreed. "Care to tell me how you escaped your own quarters?"

"Maybe I came up with such a good distraction they never even saw me leave."

Kaidyn raised an eyebrow.

"Or maybe I seduced one of the guards," Luck continued, batting his eyelashes in an unconvincing display of flirtatiousness. "Hinted at my many charms."

"Really."

"Oh, all right. Someone did show off their charms, but it wasn't me. I called in a favor from a friend. A very well-endowed friend, if you must know."

"Ah. That makes more sense." Luck's particular brand of roguish appeal had always made him popular with women, though this one might have been anything from a passing acquaintance to a lover. He often visited the brothels and was familiar with many of the workers there, men and women both.

"I'll have you know I happen to be very seductive when I put my mind to it."

"I'm sure."

Luck grinned again, pushing unruly curls from his eyes.

Though Kaidyn didn't say it, he had missed his childhood friend. Now that they were separated by different training schools, it had been several weeks since their last meeting.

As far as Kaidyn was concerned, Luck had been one of the sole joys to result from moving permanently to the capital as a child. The looming threat of war with Iskandir had finally become serious enough for the family to abandon their less grand yet far more private summer palace in the north. By comparison, the capital had seemed overly large and unfriendly. Even his sister, whom Kaidyn had idolized, appeared to grow cold and remote almost overnight.

The other children living in and around the palace were minor relatives and little lords or ladies in their own right. They took cues from their elders and kept their distance from him. Everyone was aware that although Kaidyn was a prince, he was unable to inherit, even had he been the eldest child. Anyone in good standing knew the Half-Blood would never have any significant role in matters of state or the court. His father's ancestry saw to that.

But Luck had been as different from them as day from night. Tall and lanky, he was a slightly wild boy even then with his head of shorn, tight brown curls and laughing eyes almost exactly the same shade as Kaidyn's own. If not for his distinctly rough manner of speech, they might even have passed as brothers. Certainly Kaidyn resembled Luck far more than he did Lyrah, who was as small as her mother, but had inherited her late father's slenderness and sea-green eyes. Kaidyn had been in awe of his new friend, so different from any other he had known and with an unquestionable talent for getting into trouble—and usually for skipping neatly out of it again.

They had been utterly inseparable in their youth. As children they had been thick as thieves and cared nothing for their difference in status. When they were together, Kaidyn, the son of the queen, was equal to Luck, the son of an undercook who worked somewhere in the palace's vast kitchens.

As the years passed, however, they experienced a growing awareness of who and what they were in the eyes of the court. They made a pact not to care about status and shared a friendly rivalry, fighting over which of them could run quicker, ride faster or fight harder.

As young men on the verge of adulthood, they had for a brief time become lovers in the way many others did who trained or fought away from home. Now, they were closer to brothers again, protective and goading in equal measures, and determined to fight the world together.

Luck was still catching his breath as Kaidyn cast a glance from their makeshift hiding place. He could neither see nor hear any sign of pursuit, though no doubt at least one or two of his instructors were among the crowd somewhere, attempting to track him down like some runaway child. Well, they would be searching a long time. Kaidyn had no intention of returning until much later, long after darkness had fallen and he would not be bothered by anyone.

With some luck, he might even be able to sleep a few hours, uninterrupted by others and his ugly thoughts. Even in the light of day they had a habit of stealing into his head, making his gut turn sour, his hands curl into fists —

"C'mon, I need a drink." Luck pushed himself back from the door frame. "On you this time. I'm your dashing savior, after all, helping you break out of there like the delicate young flower you are."

Kaidyn grunted but nodded, even as an unwelcome sense of responsibility nagged at him. He was, despite everything, a son of the royal family as well as a soldier, and his actions reflected on them. He shouldn't be worrying his mother, shaming his sister, giving the Council yet another reason to despise him by shirking his duties.

"You're doing it again." Luck jostled him playfully, scattering his thoughts.

"Doing what?"

"Overthinking it."

Kaidyn made a conscious effort to relax his shoulders and allowed Luck to sweep them back out into the milling throng. They walked at a slower pace, the crowd swarming around Kaidyn as he trailed behind Luck, who led the way to one of their frequent drinking spots. It was not the first time they had passed an evening in such a way — and it would almost certainly not be the last.

But Kaidyn could not fault Luck for trying to distract him and knew that however isolated he might feel, he was not alone in his sense of entrapment. It was like a noose, one that gradually tightened day by day as empty, faceless spectators hissed and jeered. They spat on him, just as they spat on Luck for being somehow lesser than they were in the world. Nobody ever bothered to say less what exactly, but Kaidyn already knew without having to be told.

Less noble. Less worthy. Less honorable. A half-breed, with the blood of an enemy nation flowing through his veins. It would have been one thing simply to be unGifted, as many nobles were no matter how high their rank. It was quite another to be a physical reminder to all who looked upon him of his race.

But for all that, he was no noble's pet to whimper and cower, or worse, beg in an effort to please or placate his so-called betters. He would turn on his masters and sink his teeth into their flesh before such a day ever came.

Suddenly aware his fingernails had been digging into his palm again, Kaidyn let out a breath in an explosive sigh. At least the tavern would be loud enough that he wouldn't be able to hear himself think. What was one more drink to try and make him forget for a time?

And so he pushed the uninvited thoughts away and followed Luck further into the crowd.

ABOUT THE AUTHOR

Diana is a New Zealand M/M romance author currently residing in New York. However, she has also lived and worked for several years in Japan and several months in Thailand. She has no idea where in the world she'll be this time next year and is pretty okay with that. Other than reading and writing, her main passions include international travel, amateur photography and competitive swimming.